BEYOND LOSS

Jacques Chambers

Table of Contents

CHAPTER 1

Daniel Thompson never imagined that life could disintegrate so completely, and with such brutal swiftness. Just a few months ago, he had everything he thought he needed: a wife, two children, and a life that, while modest, was at least steady. He was no stranger to hard work, and never had been. Every morning, well before the first light of dawn cut through the night sky, Daniel would lace up his worn-out work boots—scuffed from years of daily wear—and pack his thermos with strong, black coffee, the only thing that kept him going some days. Then, he'd head out to do the kind of work most people never even noticed, let alone appreciated. He cleaned the spaces that others simply passed through without a second thought: grimy apartment buildings, dingy hotels, sterile office spaces. Daniel had scrubbed the floors, emptied the trash, and wiped the dust from places where nobody else ever cared to look. He understood that his work wasn't glamorous; in fact, it was far from it. But that didn't matter to him. It was honest labor, and it kept his family afloat. It put food on the table, even if the meals weren't extravagant. It bought his kids, little Sophie and Mason, the clothes they needed for school and kept a solid roof over their heads, a roof that Daniel had once been proud of.

But now, that roof no longer belonged to him. His wife, Beth, had found someone else—someone younger, someone who hadn't yet been worn down by the daily grind, someone whose face still held the smoothness of youth and whose eyes hadn't dulled with exhaustion. Beth hadn't been vicious about it, not exactly. But the way she explained herself, the carefully chosen words she used to end it all, stuck with Daniel like a dull, constant ache that gnawed at him. They weren't the words of anger, but of indifference. That, perhaps, was worse.

"It's not working anymore, Daniel. I'm not happy," Beth had said, her voice eerily calm as she stood in the kitchen, arms crossed tightly over her chest as though she were steeling herself for the chaos she was about to unleash. Her words were simple, but they cut through him with brutal efficiency. The house, once alive with the sounds of kids playing, their laughter bouncing off the walls, suddenly felt cold and unfamiliar—like it belonged to someone else entirely. "You need to leave."

There had been no room for negotiation, no hint of hesitation in her voice. Beth didn't ask him to understand, didn't offer any explanation beyond her carefully measured words. Her tone had been flat, final, as though this was just another item on her to-do list that needed checking off. Daniel stood there, blindsided, trying to make sense of it. He'd known their marriage wasn't perfect; they'd had their share of arguments, moments of silence that lingered too long. But he didn't think it had come to *this*. He thought the hard work he put in—the long hours, the sleepless nights, the constant hustle to make sure their bills were paid on time—meant something. He'd pushed himself to his limits to shield his children from the weight of adult worries, making sure Sophie and Mason didn't have to feel the strain of the life he and Beth had built. But apparently, none of that mattered anymore. Beth was done. She wanted out. And as if that wasn't enough to completely dismantle his world, the universe decided to twist the knife. On the same day, just hours after Beth had delivered her verdict, Daniel lost his job. The small cleaning company he had worked for, the one that barely kept their heads above water most months, had been absorbed by a larger corporation. The new owners had no interest in keeping Daniel or any of his coworkers on board. It wasn't personal, just business. No severance package, no advanced warning. A five-minute meeting followed by a hollow handshake that meant absolutely nothing. His entire life—his marriage, his family, his job—had disintegrated in the span of a few hours.

Now, Daniel was left with nothing and nowhere to go. His savings were a joke—barely enough to scrape by for a month, let alone cover the deposit on an apartment. And that was before Beth had tangled him in the legal web of their separation. The court had ordered him to pay child support for Sophie and Mason, which he wanted to do—he loved his kids and would do anything for them—but the reality was, every penny he earned was already gone before it even touched his hands. What little financial security he had left was devoured by legal fees and monthly payments that left him with nothing for himself.

Daniel had no family in the city, no safety net to fall back on. His parents had passed years ago, and while he had a brother, he might as well have been on the other side of the world. His brother had his own life, his own responsibilities, and lived states away, too preoccupied with his own family to even notice the wreckage of Daniel's. The isolation was suffocating; the silence in his own life, deafening.

With nowhere else to turn, Daniel found an unlikely refuge in the very place he had once cleaned on occasion: a local church. It was a building he knew well, though his relationship with it had always been purely transactional—another job, another place to scrub floors and empty trash bins. But now, it was something more. The pastor, Reverend Marshall, was a soft-spoken man with kind eyes that seemed to cut right through Daniel's façade the moment he walked in, shoulders slumped, face etched with exhaustion. Reverend Marshall didn't need to ask questions; he had seen that look of quiet desperation before. Without hesitation, he offered Daniel a place to stay, a temporary reprieve from the chaos of his unraveling life. The room was small, tucked away behind the church's main sanctuary, barely more than a storage space. It held a cot, thin and hard but better than the street, a window that seemed stuck in a half-closed position, and a nightstand with a worn Bible sitting on top, its cover frayed from years of use. The space was sparse, nothing more than the bare essentials, but it was more than Daniel could have asked for, more than he thought he deserved at this point. At night, after the church emptied out and the last of the congregation's footsteps faded into the distance, the silence in that room became both a blessing and a curse. He would lie on the cot, staring at the cracked ceiling, listening to the distant hum of the city that never fully slept—the occasional rumble of a car, the sharp wail of a siren slicing through the otherwise still night air. These sounds became a soundtrack to his thoughts, which seemed impossible to escape. He would think about what his life had been just a few months ago and what it had become now, how everything had unraveled so quickly and so completely. On some nights, the pressure of it all would drive him out of that small room, and he'd find himself walking the deserted streets around the church, as if moving through the city's emptiness could offer him some semblance of control, some direction, even if he had nowhere to go. The city at night felt different—quieter, stripped down to its bones in the absence of daylight. As Daniel wandered, he passed by old brownstone buildings with their iron fences and darkened windows, silent witnesses to a life that felt foreign to him now. He couldn't help but wonder what stories were hidden behind those walls. Did anyone living there know what it was like to lose everything in the span of a single day? Did they understand the kind of hollowness that settled in your chest when your family was gone, your job taken, your sense of self obliterated?

During the daylight hours, Daniel worked for the church, taking up the same kind of tasks that had filled his life before— cleaning, scrubbing, polishing. He knew this work; it was familiar, and in some ways, that familiarity was grounding. He scrubbed the marble floors of the sanctuary until they gleamed in the fractured light that filtered through the stained-glass windows. He cleaned the pews, making sure each one was spotless for the next service, polished the wooden altar until it shone, and swept the small courtyard where the congregation would gather after Sunday worship. The physical labor gave him something to focus on, a way to keep his hands busy even if his mind was still storming. But as much as the work gave him a routine, it wasn't enough to quiet the constant noise in his head. The gnawing questions, the endless replay of what had gone wrong and why. The anger, the regret, the confusion—they were always there, no matter how hard he scrubbed, no matter how much he tried to lose himself in the repetition of his tasks.

He thought about his kids constantly, as if their presence in his mind was the only thing keeping him tethered to some semblance of stability. Sophie, with her big brown eyes that seemed to absorb the world in a way that was both innocent and knowing, and her wild, untamed hair that never quite stayed in place, no matter how much Beth tried to tame it. She had always been a little firecracker, full of questions and boundless energy, a force that brought light to every corner of Daniel's life. And then there was Mason—his boy—just beginning to find his footing in the world, still young enough to see his father as a hero. Mason had just started learning to play baseball, that little glove too big for his small hands, but he'd throw his heart into every swing, every catch, looking up at Daniel for approval. Those moments felt like a lifetime ago.

Daniel missed their laughter more than anything—the unrestrained, joyful sound that used to echo through the house. The sound of their feet pattering across the hardwood floors, racing from room to room in that chaotic way kids do when the world is still a playground and the future is nothing to worry about. But that house was no longer his home. Now, the laughter was gone, and he only saw Sophie and Mason on weekends, their once joyful reunions growing more awkward with each passing visit. The uncomfortable silences that now stretched between them were a painful reminder that their family was fractured, and no matter how much he tried to hide it, his children could sense the change. They were adjusting to a new reality, one where Dad didn't live with them anymore, and it stung Daniel every time he saw the subtle signs—Mason hesitating to call him "Dad" the same way he used to, Sophie avoiding eye contact when they talked about the house or Beth.

Beth had moved on with unnerving speed, and Daniel knew, in that way you just know without needing confirmation, that she was living with the new guy. He didn't know the details, didn't care to know. Every mention of her new life made him nauseous, like a knot twisting tighter in his gut. It was bad enough that she had tossed him aside like an old shirt—something worn out and no longer useful. But the idea that she was already building a new life, starting fresh with someone else, made him sick in ways he couldn't quite put into words. He tried not to let the anger consume him. She was still the mother of his children, and for their sake, he couldn't afford to hate her, not openly. But in those quiet moments, when he was alone in that tiny backroom at the church, the bitterness crept in like a slow poison. He was the one sleeping on a thin cot, scrubbing floors for a living, while Beth had moved forward without a second glance, as if the life they had built together had never really mattered. There were nights, though, when the anger faded, leaving only a cold, empty numbness in its place. Those were the hardest nights, when he felt like a ghost, going through the motions of his own life but not truly living it. He had never been a particularly religious man. Sure, he believed in something—a vague notion that there was more to life than just what you could see—but he wasn't the type to pray, not before all of this, and certainly not now. He hadn't come to the church for salvation; he came because he had nowhere else to go. But as the days dragged on, as he woke up to the same view of the cracked ceiling and the same thin light filtering through that stubborn window, he found himself glancing more and more at the Bible on the nightstand. It sat there, day after day, its frayed cover and yellowing pages untouched. He didn't open it—he wasn't ready for that—but just seeing it was enough to make him wonder if maybe, just maybe, there was something beyond the wreckage of his current life.

Reverend Marshall had noticed, of course. The pastor would check in from time to time, never pushing too hard, but always offering a kind word, a moment of quiet conversation. A couple of times, he had gently suggested that Daniel might want to talk, or pray, or at least share what was on his mind. But Daniel always declined, keeping his distance. It wasn't that he didn't appreciate the offer. He did. Reverend Marshall was a good man, and in a world where everything felt hollow and meaningless, Daniel could at least respect that. But the truth was, Daniel wasn't sure he had anything left to say. What was the point of praying when you didn't even know what you were praying for? When you couldn't find the words to describe the emptiness inside you? So instead, Daniel kept scrubbing floors, kept sweeping courtyards, and kept going through the motions. Because what else was there to do?

Nights in the church were anything but peaceful. Daniel had hoped they might be, at least in the beginning. He figured that in a place meant for people to lay down their burdens, where they came to feel closer to something larger than themselves, the quiet would offer some kind of solace. A sanctuary in more ways than one. But instead, the silence in that backroom was suffocating, as though the very walls were pressing in on him. The wooden floorboards creaked with each subtle shift in the night, their groans amplified by the stillness. Even the faint hum of the city outside—distant traffic, the occasional blare of a siren—felt sharp and invasive, cutting through the dark like unwelcome intruders. Every sound seems louder here, more pronounced, as if the universe refused to let him forget his isolation, his failure. He would lie awake on the thin cot, staring up at the cracked ceiling, his eyes following the faint trails of moonlight that crept through the narrow, half-open window. The nights were long, drawn out, and filled with the kind of thoughts he couldn't escape from, no matter how much he tried. He would lie there, wondering how everything had fallen apart so quickly. It wasn't just the loss of his job or his marriage—it was the disintegration of everything he thought he understood about his life. The foundation he had spent years building, steady and secure, was now a pile of rubble, and he couldn't figure out where he had gone wrong.

He had always been a provider. That's what defined him. Not flashy or full of ambition, but reliable, steady—he prided himself on that. He wasn't the kind of man who made grand gestures or chased after some elusive dream. He kept his head down, did his work, and took pride in getting the small things right. He was never late for a shift, no matter how grueling the day before had been. The bills were always paid on time, even if it meant picking up extra hours to make sure of it. His kids never went without. Sophie always had new clothes for school, and Mason's baseball gear was always the best he could afford. Even when things got tight, he found a way to make it work. And while he and Beth had their problems—moments of tension that stretched between them like a taut wire—he'd always figured they were just going through the motions, like so many couples do. He assumed they'd come out the other side eventually, still standing, still together. You don't just walk away from over a decade of shared life, of kids, of memories. Not for no reason. At least, that's what Daniel had believed. But Beth had walked away. And now, as he lay there in the stillness of the church, replaying every moment in his mind, he couldn't help but question everything he thought he knew. Maybe he hadn't been enough. Maybe all the long hours and extra shifts meant nothing in the end. Maybe while he was out there trying to provide, Beth had been slipping further and further away, and he just didn't see it. The thought gnawed at him in the quiet hours of the night, turning over in his mind until he couldn't tell where the anger ended and the self-doubt began.

But now, surrounded by nothing but the cold, unfeeling walls of the church, Daniel began to understand that he had been wrong about a lot of things. He had missed the cracks that had been forming, slowly but surely, in the foundation of his marriage. He had been too distracted by the grind, by the relentless need to provide, that he hadn't noticed the subtle shifts in Beth. He hadn't seen the way her smile had started to fade when she looked at him, how it no longer reached her eyes. He hadn't paid enough attention to the way she stopped asking about his day, how her casual "How was work?" had turned into silence, or how she seemed less interested in his answers when she did ask. There were so many signs he should have seen—the late nights out with her friends, the increasing distance between them, the way they lived under the same roof but hardly spoke anymore. He realized now that there had been months, maybe even years, where they had merely existed alongside each other, two people living separate lives in the same house, their connection eroding with each passing day.

Still, despite all that, Daniel had always assumed they'd find a way to work through it. He had believed, in that steadfast, unquestioning way, that marriage was about enduring the tough times, staying even when it felt impossible. He thought that was what you did. You held on, even if it meant clinging to a sinking ship, because that's what being married was supposed to mean. But Beth… she had decided otherwise. She had chosen to let go. He remembered the day she told him to leave as if it had just happened. The memory played itself over and over in his mind, the details so sharp and vivid that it felt like he was reliving it every time he closed his eyes. The house had smelled like coffee and toast that morning. Sophie and Mason were still in their pajamas, curled up on the couch with a cartoon playing too loudly in the background. It was just a regular morning, the kind that had been so familiar to him that he hadn't noticed how fragile it had become. He had just come home after an early morning shift, scrubbing floors in one of those downtown office buildings, his body aching from the hours of labor, but there had been a certain comfort in coming home. Home was supposed to be where he could rest, where he could see his kids' faces and feel like the hard work was worth something. It was his refuge.

But that warmth, that sense of home, had vanished the moment Beth spoke. There had been no warning, no preamble. Her words had cut through the air like a knife, and in that moment, everything he had taken for granted—his family, his life—began to crumble around him. Beth hadn't minced her words. She looked him dead in the eyes and said she wasn't in love with him anymore. No softening of the blow, no gentle letdown. She had already met someone else, a younger man she'd crossed paths with through mutual friends. Daniel had stood there, blindsided, his mind reeling as he struggled to process what she was telling him. How had this happened? Where had he been while she was falling for someone else? The weight of her words pressed down on him like a physical force, but still, he didn't yell. He didn't plead for her to reconsider. His voice remained lodged in his throat, thick with shock and disbelief, as though the reality of it all was too much for him to even speak against. That same afternoon, Beth had packed his things. She moved through the house, folding his clothes and stuffing them into suitcases like it was just another task to check off her list. It was mechanical, detached. Daniel barely had time to think before he found himself standing on the front porch, two battered suitcases at his feet, the door closed behind him with a finality that felt like it had been waiting for this moment all along. The house he had lived in, loved in, the place where he had tucked his kids into bed, shared meals with his family, and planned a future that now seemed like a distant dream, had shut him out for good. He stood there for what felt like hours, rooted to the spot, staring at the front door. His door. Or at least, it had been.

Now, he was here. *St. Jude's Chapel*, an old stone church that had become the closest thing to shelter he had. The building itself was modest, its faded white steeple looming over the worn-out neighborhood like a silent, forgotten guardian. It stood at the corner of a block that had seen better days, just like Daniel. The stained-glass windows that once depicted saints in vibrant colors had grown dull with age and neglect, some of them cracked, the scenes now distorted and incomplete. The chipped stone facade was a fitting reflection of how Daniel felt—weathered, crumbling at the edges, but still standing, somehow. The streets surrounding the church weren't busy. Occasionally, a pedestrian would hurry past, eyes down, focused on wherever they needed to be. A few streets over, the distant sound of children playing would drift on the wind, but it felt far removed from the quiet, almost desolate atmosphere that clung to the church. The neighborhood wasn't dangerous, but it wasn't inviting either. Some of the nearby buildings had boarded-up windows, their paint peeling, long abandoned to time and decay. Graffiti covered the alleyways, the vibrant tags and messages like defiant protests against the neglect. It was the kind of place you passed through, not where you stopped.

And that was fine with Daniel. He found comfort in the anonymity. Here, nobody knew him, and more importantly, nobody cared. There were no prying eyes, no whispered gossip, no one to ask uncomfortable questions about what had happened to the man who used to be a husband, a father, a provider. He was just another nameless figure in a forgotten part of the city, and for now, that was enough. Daniel would often find himself sitting alone in the sanctuary during the late afternoon hours, long after he'd finished cleaning for the day. The place was silent except for the creak of old wood or the occasional sigh of the wind rattling the stained glass. There was something haunting about the emptiness of it all. Sometimes, Reverend Marshall would find him there, sitting in one of the back pews, staring ahead, lost in his own thoughts. The Reverend, with his slow, deliberate movements, would sit down beside him, but he never spoke right away. It was always as though he was waiting for Daniel to make the first move.

One evening, when the dimming light cast long shadows across the floor, Daniel broke the silence.

"Do you think some people just aren't meant to make it?" His voice came out rough, the words heavy with everything he'd been holding inside. "I mean, really make it. Maybe... maybe some of us are just meant to get by, survive, but never really live."

Reverend Marshall turned to him, his face as calm as ever, but there was a sharpness in his eyes, a depth that hinted he had seen more than his quiet demeanor suggested. After a long pause, he spoke.

"I don't think anyone is *meant* for anything, Daniel. Not in the way you're asking." His voice was low, steady, carrying the weight of years spent listening to broken souls pour out their burdens. "We live, and we survive, yes. But it's not about what we're *meant* for. It's about what we choose to do with the time we're given."

Daniel let the words hang in the air for a moment, but they didn't feel comforting. They didn't ease the ache inside him. He stared down at his hands, calloused and rough from years of hard work, from trying to provide for a family that had slipped through his fingers.

"I don't even know what that means anymore," Daniel said quietly. "Choice. What choices do I have left? My wife left me for someone else. My kids... they barely look at me the same way they used to. I'm living in a church because I've got nowhere else to go. What kind of choices are those?"

Reverend Marshall leaned forward slightly, resting his hands on his knees. His face, though compassionate, didn't soften into any of the usual empty platitudes Daniel had grown used to hearing from others. There was no false hope in his voice, no promise that things would magically get better.

"Life doesn't stop because we lose things, Daniel," he said, his eyes fixed ahead, as if seeing something beyond the walls of the church. "It doesn't stop even when the things we thought we could never live without are taken from us. Your wife, your job, even your home they're all parts of you, yes. But they don't define you. The only thing that defines you is what you do now."

Daniel shook his head, a bitter laugh escaping his throat. "And what am I supposed to do with that? Start over? At my age? I'm not some kid just out of school with the world ahead of me. I've been working for years, and for what? To end up right here, scrubbing floors again, sleeping in a backroom like I've been cast aside? What kind of second chance is that?"

Reverend Marshall didn't flinch. "It's the kind everyone gets, Daniel. Maybe not in the way you expected. Life isn't kind enough to offer us clean slates. It just keeps moving, and if we want to keep up, we have to move with it. Even when we feel like we've been left behind."

Daniel's silence hung thick between them, the words churning in his mind. He wanted to argue, to push back, but he had nothing left to give. He had been angry for so long—angry at Beth, angry at himself, angry at the world for dealing him a hand that felt so impossibly unfair. But now, sitting there in the dim sanctuary, all he could feel was exhaustion. The weight of everything was too much.

"You make it sound so easy," Daniel muttered, his voice barely audible.

Reverend Marshall shook his head. "It's not easy. It never is. But that's the point. You don't have to figure it all out today. Or tomorrow. Maybe not even next year. But every day you get up, every day you keep going, that's a step. You may not see it now, but even sitting here, asking these questions—that's something. It's a beginning, Daniel."

Daniel stared ahead, his eyes fixed on the flickering candles at the altar. He wasn't sure he believed the Reverend, wasn't sure if he could take another step, let alone keep going. But in that moment, something inside him shifted, even if only slightly. It wasn't hope, not yet. It wasn't the promise of a better tomorrow. It was just the understanding that there was more to do, more to face. Even if it felt impossible, he had to keep going, if not for himself, then for his kids.

After a long stretch of silence, Daniel finally stood up, his body stiff and tired. "Thanks," he muttered, not quite sure what he was thanking the Reverend for.

Reverend Marshall simply nodded, not expecting anything more. "Anytime, Daniel. Anytime."

Daniel walked out of the sanctuary, the weight of his life still pressing down on him, but his steps felt just a little bit lighter. He wasn't sure if anything would change, but for the first time in a long while, he allowed himself to think that maybe, just maybe, it could.

CHAPTER 2

Daniel scrubbed the marble floors of the church with an almost mechanical rhythm, his hands moving without thought, his body going through the motions as if by instinct. The brush moved back and forth, back and forth, a steady, monotonous beat that mirrored the droning in his mind. There was something maddening about it, the endless repetition, the feeling that no matter how hard he worked, the dirt would never really go away. He could spend hours scrubbing one spot, and when he looked back, it would still feel like there was something left—a shadow, a mark, something he couldn't quite reach. It reminded him too much of his life, of the mistakes he couldn't undo, the things he couldn't fix. He wiped the sweat from his brow, letting out a long sigh as he leaned against the wooden handle of the mop. The church was empty, save for the flickering of candles near the altar. The stained-glass windows cast muted colors onto the floor, soft blues and reds mixing together in abstract patterns. Daniel had never noticed how beautiful the light was in this place before, not when he was too busy keeping his head down, focused on the grime beneath his feet.

But the beauty of it didn't soothe him. Not today.

The thoughts gnawed at him, insistent, like a dull ache in the back of his skull.

What now?

It was a question he had asked himself a thousand times, and still, he didn't have an answer. The world had pulled the rug out from under him, and he was still reeling, trying to find his balance, but the ground wasn't there. Everything that had once given his life purpose and structure was gone, torn away so swiftly it was like a bad dream. His marriage—gone. His home—gone. His job—gone. And his kids… his heart ached the most for them.

Sophie and Mason. The thought of them was a knot in his chest, tightening every time he pictured their faces. Sophie had his eyes, the same deep brown that looked too serious for a child. Mason had Beth's smile, bright and full of life, the kind that made you think the world was still a good place. They were the only real thing left in his life, but even they felt like they were slipping through his fingers.

He wasn't their rock anymore. He wasn't the man who tucked them in every night, the one who knew their bedtime routines, their favorite stories, the way they liked their pancakes cut into funny shapes in the morning. Now, he was the parent they saw on weekends, the one who picked them up and dropped them off, trying to act like everything was okay when it wasn't. There was a distance growing between them, one that scared him more than anything. Sophie didn't talk as much when she was with him anymore, and Mason—Mason seemed like he was just waiting for Daniel to prove he wasn't the dad he used to be. Daniel straightened up, tossing the mop into the bucket with more force than necessary, the loud clatter echoing in the empty church. He walked toward the back pew and sat down, elbows on his knees, head in his hands. He stared at the floor beneath him, the same floor he'd just spent hours cleaning, and yet, it didn't look any different. The grime was still there. The shadows still lingered. A part of him wondered if this was it. If this was what the rest of his life was going to be—scrubbing floors, living in the backroom of a church, trying to piece together a life that had shattered into too many pieces to ever make whole again. He had never been one for self-pity. He was a provider, a worker. He took the bad days and moved forward. But now, with nothing solid beneath him, with no direction, it was hard to see a way out. Hard to see anything except the mess his life had become. His thoughts drifted back to Beth. He had loved her. He knew he hadn't been perfect—no one was—but he had done his best. Or at least, he thought he had. Looking back, he could see the cracks now, the ones he had ignored for too long. The way she had grown distant, the way their conversations had become shorter, colder. But he had convinced himself that they'd make it through. That's what marriage was, right? You stuck it out, even when it got hard. But Beth hadn't seen it that way. She had moved on, found someone new, someone younger, someone who wasn't worn down by years of working just to keep their family afloat. And Daniel... Daniel was left standing outside their house with nothing but a couple of suitcases and a lifetime of memories that didn't mean a damn thing anymore.

"What am I supposed to do now?" Daniel muttered to himself, his voice barely more than a whisper, swallowed by the vast emptiness of the church.

As if in response, the door at the far end of the sanctuary creaked open. Reverend Marshall stepped in, his soft footsteps echoing down the aisle. He noticed Daniel sitting in the back, his usual calm demeanor betraying a hint of concern.

"Daniel," the Reverend called, his voice cutting through the silence. "I've been looking for you."

Daniel didn't respond at first, just kept staring at the floor, lost in the weight of his thoughts. Reverend Marshall sat down beside him, not too close, but near enough that Daniel could feel the presence of someone who wasn't expecting anything from him.

"You've been working hard," the Reverend said after a moment. "But you look like you've been carrying something heavier than a mop."

Daniel let out a slow breath, shaking his head. "What's the point?" he asked, his voice flat. "I clean these floors every day, but they're never clean. The dirt never goes away. No matter how much I scrub, it's still there."

Reverend Marshall leaned back slightly, resting his hands on his knees. "Sometimes, Daniel, it's not about making things perfect. It's about keeping things from getting worse. The dirt might always be there, but you're still making a difference, even if you can't see it."

Daniel clenched his jaw. "It doesn't feel like it. Not here. Not in my life. I've lost everything that mattered. I'm just... going through the motions. I don't even know what I'm doing anymore."

The Reverend nodded slowly, letting Daniel's words settle in the air. He didn't rush to fill the silence, didn't offer hollow reassurances. Instead, after a long pause, he spoke in a voice as gentle as it was firm.

"You're still here, Daniel. You're still breathing, still fighting. That counts for something."

Daniel shook his head, not ready to believe it. "I don't feel like I'm fighting. I feel like I'm just waiting for everything to finish falling apart."

Reverend Marshall placed a hand on his shoulder, not in a gesture of comfort, but more like an anchor, something steady in the storm Daniel was caught in. "Maybe you don't see it yet, but getting up every day, facing it all—that's a fight, Daniel. It's not always the big things that matter. Sometimes, it's just about keeping your head above water."

Daniel stared at the floor, the weight of the Reverend's words pressing against his chest. He wanted to believe it. He wanted to believe that maybe, just maybe, there was still something left worth fighting for. But it was hard—so damn hard—to see past the wreckage of his life.

"I don't know if I have it in me," Daniel finally said, his voice barely audible.

Reverend Marshall gave his shoulder a light squeeze before standing up. "You don't have to know right now. Just keep going, one day at a time. That's all you can do."

And with that, the Reverend walked back down the aisle, leaving Daniel alone again with his thoughts. But this time, the silence felt a little less suffocating, a little less empty.

Daniel sat on the edge of the cot, staring at his hands, rough from years of work, but now they felt useless. What good were they if he couldn't even hold his own life together? The thought of Sophie and Mason gnawed at him constantly. They were still so young, innocent, and full of hope. They didn't deserve this. They didn't deserve to be the ones stuck in the middle of something they never asked for. He hated himself for it. What kind of father am I now? The question circled his mind like a vulture.

He couldn't answer it, and that was the part that crushed him the most. When Sophie hugged him tightly, her small arms wrapping around his neck as if she could hold him together, he felt the weight of his failure. Mason, too—always looking at him with those bright eyes, waiting for Daniel to say something that would make sense of it all. But Daniel couldn't explain it. He couldn't tell them why he wasn't living with them anymore, why they had to visit him instead of him being there when they woke up in the morning.

One Saturday evening, as he was dropping them off at Beth's new place, Sophie lingered in the backseat of the car longer than usual. Daniel turned to look at her, forcing a smile as he reached to unbuckle her seatbelt.

"You okay, kiddo?" he asked softly, his voice trying to be cheerful but coming out tired.

Sophie nodded, but her eyes told a different story. She was quiet for a moment, fiddling with the hem of her jacket, her small hands moving restlessly. "Dad... why don't you come home anymore?"

Daniel froze. He had known this question would come eventually, but he wasn't ready. How could he be? He swallowed, his throat tightening as he tried to think of something—anything—that wouldn't break her heart.

He leaned back in his seat, running a hand through his hair. "It's... complicated, Soph," he said, his voice barely above a whisper. "Your mom and I—we just... we decided it's better this way."

Sophie's brow furrowed, her lips pressing into a thin line. "But why? Don't you want to be with us anymore?" Her voice cracked on the last word, and Daniel felt his chest tighten.

"Of course, I do," Daniel said quickly, reaching out to gently take her hand. "I love you and Mason more than anything in the world. This isn't about not wanting to be with you. It's just... sometimes, grown-ups don't always figure things out the way they should. And I know it's hard to understand right now, but it doesn't mean I don't care. I'm still here, Soph. I'll always be here."

Sophie stared at him for a long moment, her eyes searching his face as if she was trying to decide whether or not to believe him. "But you're not there. Not really."

Daniel felt the words hit him like a punch to the gut. He wanted to tell her she was wrong, to reassure her that everything would be okay. But she wasn't wrong. He wasn't there, not the way he used to be. And he couldn't promise her that things would ever go back to how they were.

"I know," he said, his voice low, thick with guilt. "I'm trying, kiddo. I really am."

Sophie looked down at her lap, silent again, and Daniel felt the shame settle deeper in his chest. How could I let this happen? He thought about Mason, too—how his son had been quiet the entire ride, staring out the window like he was somewhere else entirely. Mason had always been the quieter of the two, but since the separation, he'd grown even more distant. It was like he didn't know how to talk to Daniel anymore, and Daniel didn't know how to reach him.

As they walked to Beth's door, Daniel held both their hands, forcing himself to smile, trying to be the dad they needed. He watched them disappear inside, Mason barely glancing back, and Sophie giving him one last look, her eyes full of questions he couldn't answer. When the door closed behind them, Daniel stood there for a moment, staring at the empty porch. The cold autumn air stung his face, but it wasn't enough to shake the heaviness that clung to him. He wanted to cry, to scream, to do something to let out the frustration, the sadness, the anger. But he couldn't. He had to keep it together, at least for their sake. He walked back to his car, feeling the weight of the silence as he drove back to the church, back to the life that felt more like a punishment than a refuge.

The next day, as he cleaned the church floors, Reverend Marshall noticed the look on Daniel's face, the way he seemed lost, detached from the world around him.

"You're thinking about them, aren't you?" the Reverend asked, his voice calm, understanding.

Daniel stopped scrubbing for a moment, staring at the floor as if the answer was written in the streaks of water on the tile. "Yeah," he muttered. "All the time."

The Reverend walked closer, standing beside him, not saying anything for a moment. Finally, he spoke, his voice soft but deliberate. "You're still their father, Daniel. Even if you're not in the same house, you're still their dad. And that means something."

Daniel shook his head, gripping the mop tighter. "Does it? I'm not there for them the way I should be. I don't even have a home to take them to. What kind of father is that?"

Reverend Marshall's eyes softened, his gaze steady on Daniel. "Being a father isn't about the house you live in or the things you can give them. It's about the love you have for them, the way you show up, even when you feel like you can't. It's about being there, in whatever way you can."

"But it's not enough," Daniel said, his voice breaking. "It's never going to be enough."

The Reverend placed a hand on his shoulder, a firm, grounding gesture. "You're right. It won't ever be perfect. But you don't have to be perfect. You just have to keep trying. Keep showing up, even when it's hard. They see that, Daniel. Maybe not now, maybe not in the way you want them to, but they'll remember that you didn't give up."

Daniel looked down, his throat tight with emotion. He wanted to believe the Reverend's words, but the doubts still lingered, thick and heavy. He felt like he had already given up, in some way. And that was what scared him the most. But when the weekends were over, and the kids were gone, Daniel would sit on the steps outside the church, watching the cars pass by, feeling like a man who had been erased from his own life. It was a strange thing, being a ghost in the world you used to belong to. The city moved on around him, indifferent to his pain, to his struggles. People walked by without a second glance, lost in their own lives, their own worries. And Daniel, well, Daniel just drifted.

Daniel often sat in the pews after his work was done, staring at the flickering light cast through the stained glass. It was as if the colors had lives of their own, dancing across the floor in delicate patterns that never lasted. Reds bled into blues, greens melted into purples. He had scrubbed these floors countless times, but the light always made them look new. On some days, the quiet brought him a strange peace. The silence felt thick, heavy, like it was swallowing the noise of the world outside, and for a moment, he could almost believe that everything was going to be okay. But most days, the silence was deafening, amplifying every thought he tried to bury.

He would watch the light, feeling the tension in his chest rise, unsure of how to deal with the emptiness. Was it supposed to get easier? He wasn't sure anymore.

One afternoon, Reverend Marshall entered the sanctuary, his footsteps soft against the stone floor. He didn't say anything at first, just sat down in the pew across from Daniel, his eyes following the same path of light that Daniel had been watching.

After a long silence, the Reverend spoke. "You ever wonder what those windows have seen? How many lives have passed through here, broken or searching, hoping for something more?" His voice was low, thoughtful.

Daniel glanced at him, then back to the colors. "Yeah, sometimes," he admitted, his voice rough. "I figure a lot of people have sat right where I am now... looking for answers."

The Reverend nodded slowly. "That's the thing about places like this," he said softly. "They hold people's hopes, their fears. Every prayer, every tear—it all lingers. And yet, it's never the place that gives answers. It's the people. It's what they choose to do when they leave these walls."

Daniel's jaw clenched slightly. "I've never been much for praying. Never seemed like the kind of thing that'd fix anything."

Reverend Marshall leaned back, folding his hands in his lap. "Prayer doesn't fix things. Not the way most people think. It doesn't erase pain, doesn't mend broken marriages, or bring jobs back. But sometimes..." He paused, as if searching for the right words. "Sometimes, it helps to say things out loud, even if it's just to yourself. It clears the fog, helps you see the next step."

Daniel looked down at his hands, rough and calloused from years of labor, from holding onto things that were now gone. "I don't know, Rev," he said quietly. "It feels like there's nothing left to say. Like I'm just... empty."

Reverend Marshall studied him for a long moment. "Maybe that's the point. Maybe the emptiness isn't something to run from. Maybe it's where you start."

Daniel let the words hang in the air, but he didn't know what to make of them. How could emptiness be a beginning? It felt more like the end of everything he'd known.

"How do you start over," Daniel asked, his voice hoarse, "when it feels like everything that mattered is gone?"

The Reverend didn't answer right away. When he did, his voice was soft but firm. "One step at a time. It's not about finding some grand purpose right now. It's about surviving this moment, getting through today. And maybe tomorrow will be a little clearer."

Daniel frowned, frustration bubbling up inside him. "I don't know if I have it in me, Rev. I've already lost so much. My wife, my home… I can barely even be the father my kids need. How am I supposed to keep going when everything feels so pointless?"

Reverend Marshall sighed, leaning forward, resting his elbows on his knees. "You're right, Daniel. I'm not going to stand here and tell you that things aren't hard, or that they'll magically get better if you just believe enough. That's not how life works. But what I will tell you is this: you're still here. You're still showing up, every day. You're still fighting, even if you don't realize it."

Daniel swallowed hard, the weight of the Reverend's words settling deep inside him. He wanted to argue, wanted to push back and say that just surviving wasn't enough, that he needed more than just the strength to wake up every morning. But he stayed silent, letting the truth sink in.

"Maybe the first step isn't about fixing everything," Reverend Marshall continued. "Maybe it's just about letting yourself be here, right now, in this place. Letting yourself feel what you need to feel without trying to run from it."

Daniel stared at the light reflecting on the stone floor, the colors blurring together as his eyes stung with unshed tears. He didn't know if he believed what the Reverend was saying, but a part of him wanted to. A part of him needed to.

"I just want to be enough for them," Daniel said quietly, his voice barely a whisper. "For my kids. I don't want them to look at me and see… this. See a man who's lost everything."

Reverend Marshall's voice was gentle, but strong. "They won't see that. What they'll see is a man who didn't give up on them, even when everything else fell apart. That's what they'll remember, Daniel. That's what will matter in the end."

Daniel didn't respond. He couldn't. His throat was tight, his mind swirling with the weight of everything that had happened, everything he'd lost, and everything he still didn't know how to regain. But for the first time in a long while, he let himself sit in that silence, in that emptiness, without running from it.

Maybe Reverend Marshall was right. Maybe the emptiness wasn't something to fear. Maybe, just maybe, it was the beginning of something new.

Daniel had never thought of himself as a man who sought refuge in places like this, but here he was, drawn to the stillness that St. Jude's offered. It wasn't peace, exactly—more like a pause, a break from the relentless weight of everything outside its walls. In a way, the thick, cold stone seemed to absorb some of his turmoil, as if the church had seen enough suffering over the years to take on a bit more. There was comfort in that, a kind of shared burden that made his loneliness feel less acute, even if it was only for a few moments.

He would sometimes watch the candles flicker near the altar, small flames barely holding their ground against the drafts that slipped through the cracks in the old windows. Each light seemed fragile, but persistent, like they refused to be snuffed out despite everything. Daniel envied them. It was a strange thing to envy— a flickering candle—but it represented something he hadn't felt in a long time: resilience. The ability to stand firm in the face of overwhelming odds. In those moments of quiet, he wondered if resilience was something you were born with, or if it was something you learned after being knocked down so many times. He thought about Beth again, about her decision to leave, to start over with someone else. Maybe she had found her own form of resilience, a way to move on from a life that no longer made sense to her. But he couldn't shake the bitterness that lingered. It felt like she had abandoned ship while he was still trying to patch up the leaks. One afternoon, after scrubbing the sanctuary floors until his knees ached, Reverend Marshall approached him. His footsteps were always light, almost reverent in their softness, but there was a weight to his presence that made Daniel look up.

"Daniel," the reverend said quietly, sitting down in the pew opposite him. "You've been here a while now, and I see you working hard, doing your best. But sometimes... hard work isn't enough to heal what's broken inside."

Daniel didn't respond at first. He wasn't sure what to say. The idea of something broken inside of him felt too raw, too close to the truth he wasn't ready to face.

Reverend Marshall continued, his voice steady but compassionate. "I'm not here to preach, or to tell you what you should do. But I've seen men carry burdens they were never meant to carry alone. And I see that in you, Daniel. You don't have to say anything, but I want you to know that you don't have to carry it all by yourself."

Daniel stared at the floor, the grain of the old wood blurring in his vision. "I don't know how to... let go of it," he finally said, his voice barely a whisper. "I don't even know if I want to."

The reverend nodded, as if he understood more than Daniel had said. "That's the hardest part, isn't it? Letting go doesn't mean forgetting. It doesn't mean the pain goes away. But sometimes, it's the only way to make space for something else. Something better."

Daniel didn't know if he believed that. But for the first time in a long while, he didn't push the words away. They sat with him, heavy but not unbearable, like the weight of the church itself.

The emptiness had become an unwelcome companion, settling in his chest and making itself at home. Daniel sat there in the stillness, staring at the stained-glass windows casting muted colors onto the stone floor. His life felt like that light—faded, fractured, a reflection of something whole that he couldn't grasp anymore. Reverend Marshall approached quietly, his footsteps barely audible on the worn wooden floor. He sat down beside Daniel, not saying anything at first, just sharing the space with him. After a while, he spoke in that familiar, gentle tone.

"You're carrying a lot, Daniel," the reverend said, his eyes fixed on the altar ahead. "More than anyone should have to."

Daniel nodded, his gaze still lost in the fractured colors on the floor. "I don't know how to let go," he admitted, his voice low. "It's like... if I do, then what's left of me?"

Reverend Marshall was silent for a moment, weighing his response. When he finally spoke, his voice was calm, but there was a depth to it that made Daniel listen in a way he hadn't before.

"Letting go isn't about giving up. It's not about forgetting the things that matter to you. Sometimes, it's about making space for something new—something that can fill the gaps where the pain has been living. It doesn't happen all at once, and it doesn't make the past disappear. But it can help ease the weight."

Daniel shook his head slightly. "I don't know if I can. I've been holding on for so long... trying to keep everything from falling apart."

The reverend shifted in his seat, his thin hands clasped loosely in his lap. "It's not easy. But maybe the things that have fallen apart were never meant to stay the way they were. Sometimes, we build our lives on foundations that crack, and no amount of holding on can stop them from crumbling."

Daniel glanced at him, a bitter smile tugging at the corner of his mouth. "So what, then? I'm just supposed to start over? Build a new life from the rubble?"

Reverend Marshall's eyes met his, steady and unflinching. "Maybe not from the rubble, but with it. Your life doesn't have to look the same as it did before, Daniel. It can be different—maybe even better. But you have to give yourself the chance to believe that."

The words hung in the air between them, heavy with meaning. Daniel didn't know if he believed them yet, but something about the way the reverend spoke—calm, certain, but never forceful—made him want to believe. For the first time in a long while, Daniel didn't push the conversation away. He let it sit with him, stirring something deep within that he wasn't ready to name yet.

As Reverend Marshall stood to leave, he placed a hand on Daniel's shoulder, a simple gesture, but it carried a warmth that lingered. "Take your time," he said quietly. "No one's expecting you to have all the answers right now."

Daniel nodded, his throat tight with unspoken emotions. He watched the reverend walk back down the aisle, his figure fading into the dim light of the sanctuary. For the first time in months, Daniel felt a small shift inside him—a crack in the emptiness. It wasn't much, but it was something. And for now, that was enough.

His words echoed softly in the empty sanctuary, swallowed up by the stone walls. Daniel closed his eyes, leaning his head back against the pew, feeling the weight of everything pressing down on him. He had never been one for grand speeches, never felt comfortable spilling his heart out to anyone—not even to himself, most of the time. But here, in the quiet, the dam had cracked, and the words came out like a slow trickle.

"I thought I had it all figured out," he continued, his voice still low, almost as if he were afraid someone might hear him. "I thought if I worked hard enough, if I was a good husband, a good father… that would be enough. But it wasn't. I wasn't."

His throat tightened, and he swallowed hard, staring up at the flickering candles. The shadows they cast felt like they mirrored his life—always shifting, never quite still, always in motion but never truly clear. He took a deep breath, his chest aching with the effort to hold back the emotions that threatened to spill over.

"I don't even know who I am anymore," he admitted, his voice breaking slightly. "I don't know what's left. My kids, Beth… they've moved on. I don't blame them, but where does that leave me? What do I have left to give?"

The wind outside seemed to pick up, rattling the old doors a little louder, but the sanctuary remained still, the silence thick around him. Daniel wasn't expecting an answer—he wasn't sure he wanted one. But as he sat there, staring at the flickering light, something in him shifted. It wasn't a voice, wasn't a revelation. It was just a quiet understanding, a small, hesitant acknowledgment that he was still here. Despite everything, he hadn't completely given up.

He sighed, the sound heavy and full of years of carrying the burden alone. "I'm tired," he whispered. "So damn tired of pretending I'm okay when I'm not."

The silence greeted his words again, but this time, it didn't feel as oppressive. It felt… patient, as if the sanctuary was willing to wait for him to figure things out, no rush, no judgment. Daniel opened his eyes, the dim light of the candles still flickering before him, and for the first time in months, he didn't feel completely hollow. There was still emptiness, still pain, but somewhere in the quiet, there was also a faint glimmer of hope.

Maybe, just maybe, he wasn't as lost as he thought.

The tears kept coming, as if years of holding everything in had finally caught up with him. There was no shame in it, no guilt—just raw, unfiltered emotion. Daniel had spent so much time trying to keep everything together, for his kids, for Beth, for himself, that he had forgotten what it meant to just let go. And here, in the empty church, with nothing but the flickering candles and the faint sound of the wind outside, he finally allowed himself that release. He could feel the weight lifting from him, bit by bit, though the heaviness in his chest remained. It wasn't something that would go away in one moment of tears—it ran too deep for that. But there was a strange comfort in the release, in the vulnerability of being completely exposed to himself. As the tears slowed, Daniel wiped his face with the back of his hand, his breath shaky but steadying. He stared up at the crucifix again, the figure of Christ seeming to look down at him with a kind of quiet understanding. There was something about the image that struck Daniel differently now. He had seen it countless times since he'd come to St. Jude's, but tonight, it felt like it carried a different weight—like it wasn't just a symbol of suffering, but of endurance, of someone who had borne the unimaginable and somehow still stood.

"I don't know how to do this anymore," Daniel whispered, his voice raspy, barely audible. "I don't know how to keep going."

The words were not a plea for answers. They were simply the truth. He didn't know what the next day would bring or how he was supposed to rebuild his life from the ruins. He had lost everything that had once given him meaning—his family, his home, his sense of purpose.

But for the first time, Daniel allowed himself to accept that he didn't need to have the answers right now. Maybe that was what Reverend Marshall had been trying to tell him all along— not that faith would magically fix everything, but that it was okay not to have it all figured out. That there was grace in admitting defeat, in falling apart, because that's where the rebuilding could begin.

As he sat there, the quiet settling in around him once again, Daniel felt something stir within him. It wasn't hope, not exactly. But it was something close—something like a small flicker of light in the darkness. And maybe that was enough for now.

CHAPTER 3

The church remained still, its towering stone walls offering a sense of permanence that Daniel hadn't felt in a long time. It was as if the weight of centuries past had settled into the very air, pressing down around him but not suffocating him—instead, cradling him. For a moment, just a fleeting moment, he allowed himself to feel something he hadn't in months. Lighter. Not healed, not whole, but lighter, as if the burden he carried had shifted ever so slightly. He couldn't pinpoint what it was that caused this brief reprieve. Maybe it was the raw honesty of his breakdown, the way he had finally let himself fall apart in a space where no one could see him. Or maybe it was simply the quietness of the church itself, a stillness so profound that it swallowed his loneliness, if only for a short while. Whatever it was, it didn't feel like a miracle, and Daniel wasn't looking for one. His life was still in pieces, scattered like glass that had been shattered too many times to ever be put back together. He didn't wake up the next day with a sudden sense of clarity or purpose. The reality of his situation hadn't changed—Beth was gone, his kids were distant, and he was still living in the backroom of a church, clinging to whatever scraps of dignity he had left. But something inside him had quieted, like a storm that had momentarily passed. The days felt a little less suffocating, the nights a little less lonely. It wasn't much, but it was enough to keep him moving forward, even if he didn't know where he was headed. It was around this time that the call came. Angela Davis. Her name carried with it a flood of memories, most of them buried so deep beneath the weight of the years that Daniel had almost forgotten what she had meant to him. Angela was his high school girlfriend, the one person he had thought, at one point, he might spend his life with. But that was a lifetime ago, before the responsibilities of adulthood had pulled them in opposite directions. She had always talked about leaving town, about chasing her dreams, and eventually, she had. She'd gone off to pursue a career in fashion, and Daniel had stayed behind, tethered to a life that he hadn't chosen as much as he had fallen into it. Their paths had diverged, and they hadn't spoken in years.

The call came late, on one of those autumn evenings when the chill in the air crept in through the cracks in the old church windows. Daniel was lying on the cot in his small, sparse room, his body aching from another day spent scrubbing floors and polishing pews. His phone, an ancient flip model he had kept for its simplicity, buzzed on the makeshift nightstand beside him. The screen lit up with an unfamiliar number. He almost didn't answer it, his first instinct being to let it go to voicemail, but something made him pick it up.

"Hello?" His voice came out rough, the sound of it foreign even to his own ears. He hadn't spoken much lately, except when absolutely necessary.

There was a pause on the other end, just long enough for him to wonder if it was a wrong number. But then a voice, soft and familiar in a way that tugged at something deep inside him, broke the silence.

"Daniel?" she said. "It's Angela."

Her voice was like a time capsule, opening up memories he hadn't revisited in years. The sound of it was warm, with that gentle tone she had always had, even when they were young and the world felt wide open to them. Hearing her name, hearing her voice after all these years, sent a ripple through him—an unsettling mixture of nostalgia and surprise. For a second, he couldn't find the words to respond, as if the past and present had collided too quickly for him to process.

"Angela…" He finally managed, her name rolling off his tongue with a strange familiarity, like it had never really left him. "It's been a long time."

For a moment, Daniel didn't know how to respond. His grip tightened on the phone, and the silence stretched just long enough for him to question whether this was real. Memories of high school flooded back—walking the halls together, sneaking out to the park, dreaming of futures that never quite came to pass. But now, those memories felt like they belonged to someone else entirely.

"Angela," he finally said, his voice rough, more from surprise than disuse. "I… I didn't expect to hear from you."

"I know," she replied softly, her voice carrying a warmth that he hadn't realized he missed. "I wasn't sure you'd even pick up."

Daniel let out a breath he didn't realize he'd been holding. "Yeah, well… I guess I didn't know I needed to."

There was a pause, then Angela's voice softened even more. "How have you been? It's been a long time."

Daniel hesitated. How do you sum up years of disappointment, of losing everything you thought you'd built? He didn't want to lie, but he also didn't want to dump the full weight of his mess on her right out of the gate.

"Surviving, I guess," he said, his words clipped. "Life didn't really go the way I planned."

Angela let out a soft, knowing hum. "Yeah, it rarely does."

They fell into a conversation that felt both familiar and foreign. Angela spoke about her life—how she had moved to the city, started her own fashion line, and spent years building her career from the ground up.

"I've been doing well, I guess," she said, though there was a quiet edge to her voice that Daniel didn't miss. "The business is growing, and it's… it's everything I wanted, you know?"

"You sound like you've done pretty well for yourself," Daniel said, trying to ignore the pang of envy in his chest. "That's… that's good. Really good."

"Yeah," she replied, though something in her tone faltered. "It's been a lot. But… it gets lonely sometimes. I've been thinking a lot about the past, about people I've lost touch with. And… I don't know, I just felt like I should call."

Daniel was quiet for a moment. "I'm glad you did," he said finally. "I didn't realize how much I needed to hear a familiar voice."

When it came time for Daniel to share his story, Angela didn't interrupt, didn't try to gloss over his pain with empty words. When he told her about Beth, the divorce, losing his job, and sleeping on a cot in the back of a church, Angela didn't say things like "It'll get better" or "You'll bounce back." She didn't offer him false hope. Instead, she simply listened.

"Damn, Daniel," she whispered after a long pause. "I'm… I don't even know what to say."

"You don't have to say anything," Daniel replied, his voice quieter now, more vulnerable. "I'm not even sure why I told you all that."

"I'm glad you did," she said gently. "You've been carrying a lot on your own for too long. You shouldn't have to."

Her words hung in the air, and for the first time in a long while, Daniel felt like maybe, just maybe, someone actually understood what he was going through.

"It's been tough," Daniel admitted, running a hand over his face. "I don't even know what I'm doing anymore. I thought I could fix things, but… now I'm not sure I even know how."

Angela's voice softened again. "You don't have to have it all figured out right now. Sometimes, it's enough just to get through the day."

It wasn't long before Angela made the offer. She had space, she told him. A spare room in her apartment that he could use. She could help him get back on his feet, help him rebuild. At first, Daniel was hesitant. He didn't want to be a burden. But Angela wouldn't take no for an answer.

"You're not a burden, Daniel," she said firmly. "We all need help sometimes. And besides, I could use someone like you around."

The phone call lingered with Daniel long after it ended. He sat on the edge of the narrow cot in the church's back room, staring at the screen, half-expecting it to light up again, as if Angela's voice could somehow reach out and pull him from the dark corners of his thoughts. Her voice had been a tether, one that had reached through the years and miles to find him when he had almost forgotten what it felt like to be connected to someone. Her words, soft yet steady, had peeled away the layers of defeat that had settled on him like dust, exposing something deep inside—a small, fragile spark of hope he hadn't felt in a long time.

Could he really take her up on her offer?

The question gnawed at him, keeping him perched on that thin line between excitement and dread. The idea of leaving, of stepping outside this back room that had become both his refuge and his prison, stirred something unfamiliar in his chest. But along with that spark of hope came fear. Not the kind of fear that kept you up at night, but the slow, creeping fear of the unknown, of change, of relying on someone else when you've spent so long trying to do it all alone.

Angela had offered him a lifeline, but could he accept it? Could he really take that step? The thought of relying on her felt almost shameful, as if accepting her help was a confirmation of his own failure. She's moved on, he thought, bitterness curling in his stomach. She had her life together—a successful career, a world of her own—and here he was, a man who had lost everything, a man sleeping in the back of a church with nothing to his name but regret and a few changes of clothes. How could he walk into her life now, a shadow of the person he used to be?

The weight of his pride pressed heavily on him, a familiar burden he had carried for years. He had always been the one who fixed things, the one who provided, the one who stood strong when everything else was falling apart. But now, what was he? A man who couldn't even provide a stable home for his kids. A man who had nothing to offer but the broken pieces of a life he didn't know how to rebuild. The thought of showing that vulnerability to Angela, of letting her see just how far he had fallen, made his chest tighten.

And yet, her offer lingered in his mind, refusing to let go. She hadn't judged him. She hadn't pitied him. She had simply extended a hand, and maybe, just maybe, this was the way forward. What else did he have left? The cot beneath him creaked as he shifted, his fingers tracing the edge of the phone. His mind raced, spinning between pride and desperation, hope and fear.

He had nowhere else to go. No next step. No plan. And for the first time, he considered that maybe he didn't have to do this alone anymore.

The following week dragged on, each day stretching endlessly, like time itself had become thick and sluggish. Daniel went through the motions—cleaning the church with the same grim determination he'd always had. The work, monotonous as it was, gave him something to hold on to. He mopped the wooden floors with mechanical precision, his hands moving rhythmically, almost unconsciously. The repetition of scrubbing, wiping, and polishing was soothing in a way, a small slice of order in a life that had spun wildly out of control. He had memorized every inch of the church by now. He knew where the pews were most worn, their wood smoothed by years of use, where the floorboards creaked underfoot, and where the alcoves collected dust. The stained-glass windows, once a source of fascination with their vibrant colors, had become a backdrop to his routine, their cracks now familiar, like scars in a place meant to be perfect. But as the days wore on, the quiet nights began to press down harder. The silence, once bearable, grew heavier, and the small backroom he slept in seemed to shrink each time he lay down. The cot, hard and narrow, offered little comfort, and each night, Daniel found himself staring at the ceiling, his thoughts pulling him into darker places. He had stopped looking in the cracked mirror above the sink altogether. The man reflected there—the hollow eyes, the unshaven face, the deep-set lines of exhaustion—was someone he barely recognized.

His days were consumed by the physical labor of keeping the church clean, but at night, his mind wandered. And lately, it wandered to Angela.

Her voice still echoed in his head from their last phone call. He hadn't spoken to her again since, but the memory of her offer lingered, like a thread he couldn't quite untangle. He thought about her often—more than he would admit to himself. The life she had built, the confidence in her voice when she spoke about her work, the way she listened without pity or judgment. It had left an impression on him, one that gnawed at the edges of his thoughts when the darkness of the church swallowed the day's noise. Could he actually take that step? The question haunted him as much as it comforted him. There was no denying the pull of her offer—an escape, a way out of this stagnant life he had found himself trapped in. But there was also fear. Not of her, but of what it would mean. Accepting her help felt like admitting defeat, like acknowledging that he couldn't fix this on his own. At the same time, though, he was tired. Tired of the endless cycle of self-doubt, of pretending like he had it all under control. And in the quiet of the church, when there was no one around and nothing to distract him, Daniel started to wonder if maybe, just maybe, he didn't have to do this alone anymore.

Angela's presence in his thoughts became something he clung to—a tiny beacon in the overwhelming darkness. He didn't know what would come of it, but for the first time in months, there was something on the horizon, some distant possibility that things didn't have to stay this way. Angela called again, her timing uncanny, as if she could sense the hesitation gnawing at him. This time, there was no gentle suggestion, no tentative offer. Her voice had an edge of urgency, cutting through the quiet on the other end of the line.

"I want to help you, Daniel," she said firmly, interrupting him before he could protest. "You were there for me when I needed it, don't you remember? Back in high school, you were always the one to listen, always the one to push me forward when no one else believed in me. Let me do that for you now."

Her words reached deep, tugging at memories he had buried under the weight of the years. He could almost see them again, sitting on those old bleachers after school, the sunlight fading, their conversations about everything and nothing stretching on until dusk. Back then, their lives had been wide open, full of possibility. Angela, with her sketches and her endless ideas, had always been different from the rest. He remembered how she would pull out crumpled sheets of paper from her bag, dresses and outfits hastily drawn in the margins of her notebooks during class. She used to talk about the fashion lines she'd create, the kind of success that seemed distant but inevitable when you were seventeen and believed the world was yours to shape. And she had done it. Somehow, despite the odds, despite everything that had changed since those bleachers and those late afternoons, she had made it. And here she was, offering to help him in return, to pull him out of the pit he had fallen into. That night, as Daniel lay on the cot in the dim church room, the thin blanket barely enough to keep out the evening chill, Angela's words echoed in his head. The cracked ceiling above him seemed like a reflection of his life—broken, with no clear path to repair. He had grown used to this small room, to the sterile smell of cleaning supplies, to the sound of the church creaking and settling in the silence of the night. But the truth had settled in with Angela's call, stark and unavoidable.

This isn't living. He had known it deep down, but hearing her voice brought it to the surface. What he was doing—cleaning floors, sleeping on a cot in the back of a church—wasn't a life. It was survival. Barely that. He had clung to his pride for so long, convinced that if he just kept his head down, kept pushing through, things would somehow change. But they hadn't. He was still stuck in the same place, in the same routine, while the world moved on without him. The thought of moving in with Angela unsettled him. It felt too close to failure, too close to admitting that he couldn't fix this mess on his own. But as he lay there, staring at the ceiling, he realized something that was even harder to admit: he couldn't keep going like this. The emptiness, the loneliness, the relentless grind of trying to scrape by—it was eating him alive. And if he ever wanted to be more than this hollow shell of himself, he had to take a chance. That night, Daniel made a decision. It wasn't easy, and it didn't come with any sense of relief or triumph. It was a decision made out of necessity, out of the slow realization that maybe, just maybe, he didn't have to do this alone. Angela had extended her hand, and for the first time in a long time, Daniel was ready to reach out.

The day Daniel left St. Jude's, the world seemed to come alive in a way that felt almost surreal. The sky was a clear, piercing blue—the kind that follows a storm as if nature itself was offering a clean slate. The sun warmed his skin as he stepped out onto the sidewalk, a single duffel bag slung over his shoulder. It was all he had now, the sum of his life in a faded bag—just a few clothes, a jacket frayed at the cuffs, and the same cleaning supplies he had clung to as though they were a lifeline. As he paused for a moment, the weight of it all hit him—not the bag, not the physical burden, but the emotional gravity of leaving this place. This old church, with its towering stone walls and cracked stained-glass windows, had been a refuge when he had nowhere else to go. And now he was stepping away from it, into the uncertainty of whatever lay ahead.

Reverend Marshall stood in the doorway, hands clasped loosely in front of him, watching Daniel with an expression that carried both warmth and concern. The reverend had seen so many people come and go through these doors, each one leaving their mark on the church, just as the church had left its mark on them. But Daniel was different. He had been a fixture here, a man who kept to himself, lost in his own thoughts, but always present. And now, after everything, he was leaving.

"You know the door is always open for you, Daniel," Reverend Marshall said, his voice gentle but firm, a quiet offering in a world that rarely gave anything freely. His eyes, with their soft weariness, conveyed a deep understanding of the weight Daniel carried.

Daniel met his gaze, feeling a lump rising in his throat. He hadn't expected to feel this much emotion about leaving, but now, standing there with the church behind him, it all felt real.

"Thank you," he managed to say, his voice rough with unspoken gratitude and something more. "For everything."

There was a silence between them, not awkward, but filled with the unspoken understanding that sometimes the simplest words carried the deepest meaning. Reverend Marshall nodded once, a slow, deliberate gesture, before stepping back into the shadows of the doorway.

Daniel turned away, his boots heavy against the cracked pavement as he walked down the street. The city stretched out before him, bustling and alive in ways that felt foreign now. Cars honked, people rushed past with the weight of their own lives bearing down on them. To them, Daniel was just another figure moving through the endless current of the city's pulse. But for Daniel, each step felt like a small rebellion against the life he had left behind, a life of stagnation and survival. The street seemed unfamiliar in the way that familiar things do when seen through new eyes. It wasn't the street that had changed, it was him. His life had unraveled slowly, one thread at a time, until he found himself in that back room at St. Jude's. But now, even though his path was still uncertain, there was a quiet determination in his steps. He wasn't sure what lay ahead, but for the first time in what felt like forever, there was the possibility of something different waiting at the end of the road.

Angela lived in a different part of town—Weston Heights, an area Daniel wasn't familiar with. It was on the opposite side of the city, far removed from the faded, grimy streets surrounding St. Jude's, where time seemed to stand still, clinging to the cracks in the pavement and the hollowed-out shells of buildings. As the bus rumbled through the sprawling city, Daniel kept his eyes fixed on the window, watching the world outside shift and transform. The scenery gradually changed—first subtly, then more noticeably. The narrow, potholed streets gave way to wider, smoother roads. Graffiti-splattered walls were replaced by clean facades, and the weary faces of passersby turned to those of hurried professionals, their strides purposeful, their clothes pressed and pristine. Weston Heights wasn't luxurious, but it was a world apart from where Daniel had spent his days. The streets here felt fresher, lighter, as though they'd been scrubbed of the weariness that clung to the older districts. The buildings stood taller, their windows reflecting the afternoon sun, and even the people seemed to move differently, as if they had somewhere important to be. For a moment, Daniel wondered what it would be like to live here, in a place where the air didn't feel thick with neglect.

When the bus finally hissed to a stop, Daniel stepped off and drew in a deep breath. The air smelled different here—cleaner, almost crisp, a strange contrast to the stale exhaust fumes and bitter concrete dust that choked the streets he'd grown up on. His lungs felt clearer, and for a brief second, he allowed himself to imagine that maybe a change of scenery could cleanse more than just the air. The houses that lined the block were modest but orderly, their small, well-kept front yards bordered by trimmed hedges and dotted with patches of grass. Trees, tall and evenly spaced, lined the sidewalks, their branches swaying lazily in the soft breeze, casting dappled shadows across the path as if they'd been there for generations. Angela's apartment building came into view after a short walk from the bus stop. It was a two-story brick structure, unremarkable in its design yet strangely inviting. Ivy crept along its sides, weaving its way up the worn brick like veins of life clinging to the past. The place wasn't extravagant, but it exuded a quiet sense of comfort, a lived-in quality that hinted at years of care. It wasn't new, but someone had taken the time to make it more than just a building. It felt like a home—a far cry from the hollow, transient spaces Daniel had drifted through in recent years. Standing in front of Angela's door, Daniel found himself hesitating, his hand hovering uncertainly over the doorbell. Doubts flooded his mind, rushing in all at once like a cold wave, leaving him momentarily paralyzed. What if this didn't work out? What if he wasn't the same man Angela remembered from high school? The boy she had known back then had been full of potential, brimming with dreams and ideas. But now... now he felt like a faded version of that person, cracked and worn down by the years, by the choices he'd made. What if he was just too broken? Too damaged to make a fresh start, too far gone to be anyone worth caring about again? His breath caught in his throat, and for a brief moment, he considered turning around, walking away before he had the chance to ruin whatever fragile hope this meeting held.

Before Daniel could back out, before the doubts could overwhelm him and push him toward retreat, the door swung open.

There she was. Angela Davis.

Time had changed her, of course—it always did—but in ways that made her seem more real, more grounded. She was older now, more mature, but still unmistakably Angela. The warmth in her eyes, the same warmth that had drawn him to her all those years ago, hadn't dimmed. If anything, it had deepened, softened around the edges with experience and life's challenges. Her dark hair was pulled back in a loose ponytail, though a few rebellious strands framed her face, softening her features. She was fuller than the girl he remembered from high school, carrying a bit more weight now, but there was a confidence in her body that hadn't been there before. She wore it like armor, like she'd come to terms with who she was and didn't need the world's approval. The simple floral dress she had on hugged her curves just enough to suggest a woman who had learned to embrace her own shape. She wasn't hiding behind anything, wasn't trying to be anyone else. The dress wasn't flashy, but it suited her—unpretentious, yet full of life. And when her lips curved into a smile, it was like those years between them, all the wasted time and distance, melted away in an instant. It was the same smile that had once lit up classrooms, hallways, moments when everything felt easy.

"Daniel," she said, her voice soft but steady, as though they had last spoken yesterday rather than the many years that had passed. There was no hint of awkwardness in her tone, no questioning why he'd shown up at her door after so long. She just stood there, calm and open, the kind of person who still made room for people in her life no matter how much time had gone by. "Come on in."

For a moment, Daniel didn't move. He just stood there, staring at her, taking in the sight of her standing in the doorway. His thoughts were a mess, tangled between past and present, between the woman in front of him and the memories of who she had been. He felt like a man lost at sea, drifting for so long that he'd forgotten what solid ground felt like beneath his feet. And here she was, a safe harbor—something real, something familiar in a world that had become increasingly foreign to him.

The duffel bag slung over his shoulder suddenly felt lighter, as though the burden he'd carried for so long had loosened, just a little. He didn't have words yet, nothing he could say would match the gravity of the moment or the mix of emotions churning inside him. So, he didn't speak. Instead, he simply stepped inside, crossing the threshold into the warmth of her home, leaving the uncertainty of the streets outside. Angela's apartment was warm in a way that went beyond temperature. It had the kind of lived-in feel that came from someone who had invested themselves into making it more than just a place to sleep. It felt like it had a soul. The walls were painted a soft cream, not stark or sterile, but gentle and calming, creating a sense of quiet comfort. The furniture was an eclectic mix— vintage pieces with worn edges and modern accents that could have clashed in a lesser space, yet here they worked together seamlessly. A mid-century armchair sat beside a sleek, glass-topped coffee table, and an old-fashioned credenza hosted a minimalistic lamp, the combination speaking to Angela's ability to blend the past and present effortlessly.

Plants adorned every windowsill, their leaves lush and green, thriving in the soft afternoon sunlight that streamed through the large windows. Ferns, succulents, and ivy cascaded down from their ceramic pots, adding life to every corner. The air was tinged with the faint scent of fresh earth, as though even the plants were contributing to the warmth of the space. Daniel hadn't expected this—he hadn't expected to be comforted by something as simple as a room. But this was Angela's space, and somehow, she had managed to make it an extension of herself. One wall was dominated by a large bookshelf that was less a piece of furniture and more of a personal statement. It was packed full of fashion books, fabric swatches tucked between their pages, and design sketches pinned haphazardly to the shelves. Rolls of fabric leaned against the side, and a dress form stood in the corner, draped with the beginnings of what looked like a jacket or a gown. Daniel had always known Angela was creative—back in high school, she'd had dreams of becoming a designer, sketching outfits in the margins of her notebooks. But seeing her space now, the tangible proof of how much she had grown into herself, how she had taken that spark and turned it into something real, something solid—it hit him differently. She wasn't just playing around with ideas anymore. She had built something.

"I've got the guest room set up for you," Angela said, her voice pulling him from his thoughts. She led him down a short hallway, her footsteps light against the hardwood floor. The hallway was narrow, the walls lined with framed photos—images of people, places, moments captured in time. Some of them Daniel recognized, old high school memories frozen in glossy prints, others were unfamiliar but seemed to belong here, just like everything else in Angela's life.

The guest room was small, but like the rest of the apartment, it was cozy, thoughtfully arranged. A neatly made bed sat against one wall, its white comforter folded down crisply, inviting in its simplicity. A modest wooden dresser stood against the opposite wall, its surface bare except for a single lamp. The window overlooked a quiet side street, where the branches of a tree swayed gently in the breeze, casting dappled shadows across the room. It wasn't extravagant or luxurious, but to Daniel, it might as well have been a palace. It wasn't just a room. It was a lifeline. It was a place to stop drifting, at least for a little while.

"Thank you," Daniel said quietly, his voice almost swallowed by the space. He set his bag down on the bed, the weight of it lessened now that he was no longer carrying it on his shoulders. But the words felt inadequate, too small to express the depth of what he was feeling. How could he put into words the relief, the gratitude, the sense of being saved from himself, from the streets, from the endless cycle of uncertainty?

Angela gave a small shrug, brushing off his thanks as if it were nothing. "It's no big deal," she said, but there was something in her eyes that told a different story. A softness, an understanding that ran deeper than the casual way she spoke. She knew this was a big deal. She knew, even if she didn't say it, that for Daniel, this was more than just a place to sleep. It was a chance, a flicker of hope in the middle of all the darkness he had been carrying. Daniel swallowed hard, his throat tightening against the surge of emotion. She had always been able to see through him, even back then. And now, it seemed, she still could.

That first night in Angela's apartment, Daniel lay wide awake in the unfamiliar bed, his eyes tracing patterns in the darkness above. The ceiling, flat and featureless, seemed impossibly far away, as if the room were larger than it really was. The sheets beneath him were soft, the kind that almost whispered when you moved against them. The mattress, firmer than he was used to but comfortable in a way that felt indulgent, cradled him in a way that felt strange after months of lying on a thin, unforgiving cot. This bed, this room, this moment—it all felt foreign. But not hostile. Not like the shelters or the streets. There was something about it that felt safe. Secure, even. Outside, the city still breathed, but the sounds of it were distant, muffled by the apartment's walls. The sirens, the street noise, the hum of life that usually pressed in on him from every side—here, it was just background static, unable to touch him. The chaos of the city was out there, beyond the brick and mortar of this place, and in here, for the first time in what felt like forever, Daniel was removed from it. Separated. It was as if Angela's apartment existed in some kind of bubble, just beyond the reach of the world he had known for so long. In the next room, he could hear her. Angela was still awake, moving about quietly as she settled in for the night. There was the soft rustle of sheets, the faint creak of her bed frame, small, domestic sounds that reminded Daniel this wasn't some dream. He was really here, inside this warm space, a guest in her life. She was there, just on the other side of the wall, close enough that if he reached out, in his mind, he could almost touch her presence. It wasn't just the physical nearness that reassured him, though. It was something deeper, something he hadn't realized he needed until now.

And for the first time in a long time, Daniel didn't feel alone.

That absence of loneliness—an emotion he had become so accustomed to that it had settled in him like an old wound—felt almost foreign in itself. He didn't know what tomorrow would bring. Whether he would find work, whether he would manage to pull his life back together piece by piece, or whether this was just a temporary reprieve from the inevitable downward spiral. Uncertainty was still there, lurking in the background, like a shadow cast by a flickering light. But as he lay there, in the darkness, listening to the quiet sounds of a home that wasn't his—yet—Daniel allowed himself something he hadn't in a long time: a flicker of hope. Just a flicker, but it was enough. Enough to let him imagine, even for a fleeting moment, that maybe things didn't have to stay the way they were. Maybe, just maybe, things could get better. He didn't know how. He didn't have answers, but for the first time, the unknown didn't feel as suffocating. Wrapped in the softness of a bed that wasn't his and under a roof that had taken him in, Daniel let himself believe, if only for a second, that he could start again.

CHAPTER 4

The following days fell into a quiet, unspoken rhythm—one that Daniel hadn't realized he was craving. It wasn't much, but it was consistent. A routine. Something solid to hold onto in the midst of the uncertainty still gnawing at the back of his mind. Angela would leave each morning for her job at the boutique, offering him a small smile and a gentle reminder that he was welcome to stay as long as he needed. And Daniel would stay, taking slow, deliberate steps toward piecing his life back together in the only way he knew how—by starting small. It began with little things. At first, he would tidy up around the apartment—dusting the surfaces, wiping down the counters, making sure the dishes were clean and put away by the time Angela got home. He wasn't doing anything monumental, but for the first time in what felt like an eternity, he felt useful again. There was something deeply grounding about the simplicity of it—knowing that his efforts, however modest, were making a difference. The apartment stayed neat because of him, and that small bit of control over his surroundings brought with it a sense of calm. Control was something he hadn't felt in a long time, not since his life had spiraled out of his grasp and into chaos. But here, in Angela's quiet little corner of the world, he had found a foothold. In the mornings, the apartment came alive in a way that made Daniel pause. The pale sunlight filtered through the sheer curtains, casting soft, golden light on the cream-colored walls, making the space feel warm, almost glowing. The shadows from the furniture stretched lazily across the floor, and the plants on the windowsills drank in the light, their leaves glistening with a vibrant, green sheen. Daniel would open the windows, letting the fresh air sweep through the space, replacing the lingering humidity of the city with a crisp, clean breeze. The subtle rustling of the leaves, the distant sounds of the world outside—it all felt peaceful in a way that was foreign to him. It was strange to wake up without dread gnawing at his chest, without the familiar weight of anxiety pressing down on him. In Angela's apartment, for the first time in years, he could just breathe.

Weston Heights, Angela's neighborhood, was a far cry from the places Daniel had been drifting through. It was quiet here, removed from the noise and chaos of downtown, where he had spent so many days navigating the city's underbelly, wandering from one alley to another in search of shelter. Here, there was an order to things—a normalcy that Daniel found both foreign and comforting. The streets were lined with modest, well-kept houses, and people seemed to know each other. Neighbors waved as they passed, exchanging pleasantries. Small kids played on the sidewalks, laughing and chasing each other under the watchful eyes of parents sitting on front stoops with coffee in hand. It was all so different from the life he had known, so far removed from the cold, impersonal city streets he had once called home. And the smells—they were new, too. The sharp tang of freshly cut grass mingled with the warm, inviting aroma of brewing coffee from the café around the corner. There was the clean, almost sterile scent of laundry detergent drifting from the laundromat down the block, mingling with the occasional hint of someone's dinner being cooked in the distance. It was all a world away from the stale, musty air of the back room at St. Jude's, where the scent of mildew clung to the walls and the church pews were worn thin from years of neglect. Sometimes, as he stood by the window, gazing out at the world beyond the glass, Daniel marveled at the quietness of it all. This neighborhood wasn't loud or fast or demanding. It wasn't like the places he had been. It was steady, predictable, and that was exactly what he needed. For now, it was enough.

One evening, about a week after he moved in, the air in the apartment shifted. Angela came through the door with an energy

Daniel hadn't seen in her before—not quite explosive, but something simmering beneath the surface. There was a quiet excitement in the way she moved, a barely contained spark that made her steps quicker, her gestures more deliberate. She set her purse down on the kitchen counter, her fingers lingering on the worn leather strap as if grounding herself for what she was about to say. Daniel, sitting at the small kitchen table, cradling a chipped coffee mug in his hands, watched her with mild curiosity. The day had been quiet, like the others before it, but now something was different.

Angela turned toward him, her lips pressed together in a way that signaled she had something important on her mind. Daniel could feel the shift, a slight tightening in his chest as if bracing for whatever was coming.

"I've been thinking," she began, her voice steady but with an undertone of uncertainty. There was a tremor there, not of fear, but of hesitation, as though she wasn't entirely sure how he'd take what she was about to say. "You know my friend Claire, right? She owns a few office buildings downtown." Angela paused, gauging his reaction before continuing. "Well, she mentioned that she needs someone to take over the cleaning contract. I think it'd be a good fit for you."

Daniel's heart stopped mid-beat, then lurched forward again, picking up a nervous rhythm. For a moment, all he could do was sit there, staring at her, the silence between them stretching out longer than it should have. The chipped coffee mug felt heavy in his hands, as if it were tethering him to the earth while his mind spun out in a million different directions. Work. She was talking about work. A real job, something that could put him back on his feet again. The thing he had been avoiding since the moment he stepped into her apartment. Daniel hadn't mentioned it, and neither had Angela—until now. He'd managed to pick up a few odd jobs during his time on the streets, just enough to scrape by, just enough to survive. But real work? The kind that came with responsibility and expectations? That felt like another life, a different version of him, one he wasn't sure he could be again.

"You think I could really do that?" The words came out softer than he intended, his voice low and hesitant, as if he were testing the waters. Vulnerability cracked through his carefully constructed shell, surprising him. It was as if the question held the weight of more than just the job—it carried the doubt that had been festering inside him for so long. Could he do it? Could he be the man he used to be? Or was he too broken now, too far removed from the person he once was?

Angela stepped closer, her face softening, but there was no pity in her expression—only calm, quiet confidence. "I know you can." Her voice was steady now, no tremor, no hesitation. "It's just cleaning, Dan. You're more than capable of that. But it's a start." She leaned against the counter, her eyes never leaving his. "You need a start."

Daniel swallowed hard, looking down at the table, his fingers tracing the chipped edge of the mug. A start. It sounded so simple when she said it. A start. But the weight of it wasn't lost on him. Starting meant trying, and trying meant opening himself up to the possibility of failure. It meant confronting the man he had become, the man who had fallen so far from where he once stood. But as he sat there, listening to the quiet hum of the refrigerator, feeling the warmth of Angela's presence in the room, something inside him shifted—just slightly.

Maybe it was time. Time to stop drifting, to stop being afraid of what he had lost, and start looking for what he might still have.

Angela didn't flinch, didn't waver in her belief. "I know you can," she said with quiet but firm conviction, as if her words alone could lift the weight off his shoulders. "You were always one of the hardest-working people I knew, Daniel. Just because things didn't work out the way you planned doesn't mean you've lost that."

Her words landed heavily, reverberating in the silent space between them. He wanted to believe her, he really did. But the weight of his past, of every mistake and failure that had led him to this point, clung to him like a dark cloud, pressing down on his chest. It wasn't just the failure of his first cleaning business that haunted him, though that wound still felt raw. It was the cascade of everything that came after—the missed payments, the mounting debt, the day he was forced to close his doors for good. The humiliation of losing it all still gnawed at him, sharp and unrelenting. How could she see anything in him now, when all he saw was the wreckage of what he used to be? Yet there was something in the way Angela looked at him, her eyes steady and unwavering, that stirred something deep inside him. She wasn't just saying the words to comfort him; she genuinely believed them. She believed in him. It was a look he hadn't seen in a long time—a look that made him feel, if only for a moment, like he wasn't completely lost. That maybe, just maybe, he could be the man he used to be. A man who was capable. A man who could build something from nothing. A man who didn't crumble under the weight of his failures. Later that night, after Angela had gone to bed, Daniel found himself sitting on the couch in the dimly lit living room. The apartment was quiet, save for the occasional creak of the floorboards as the building settled. The soft, amber glow of a streetlight seeped in through the curtains, casting long, jagged shadows across the floor. Daniel leaned back, his hands clasped together, staring at nothing in particular as his thoughts churned.

He thought about his old business. The long nights spent scrubbing the floors of office buildings until his back ached and his hands were raw. The satisfaction he used to feel when he saw his reflection gleaming back at him in a spotless window, knowing that he had built something with his own two hands. He had been good at it—damn good. But life had a way of turning everything upside down when you least expected it. One bad contract, a few missed opportunities, and suddenly everything he had worked so hard for had crumbled beneath him. But now, sitting in the stillness of Angela's living room, with the echo of her words still reverberating in his mind, he felt something he hadn't felt in a long time. A flicker of hope. It was faint, fragile, barely a spark. But it was there, and that alone was enough to keep him rooted in place. Maybe it wasn't too late. Maybe he wasn't as far gone as he thought. The doubts still lingered, of course—they always would. But for the first time in what felt like years, Daniel found himself wondering if the road ahead didn't have to be as bleak as he had imagined. Maybe, with Angela's belief in him as the foundation, he could begin to build something again. It wouldn't be easy, and it certainly wouldn't happen overnight. But as he sat there, bathed in the soft light of the streetlamp, Daniel allowed himself to entertain the possibility that he might not be done yet.

Maybe it wasn't too late to start over.

The next morning, Daniel found himself standing in front of a sleek office building downtown, a place that felt like a world apart from the old motels and apartment complexes he used to clean. Claire, Angela's friend, had agreed to meet with him to discuss the contract, and now he was here, trying to ignore the knot of nerves twisting in his stomach. The building itself was modern, all glass and steel, with large windows reflecting the early morning sun. The lobby was immaculate, with polished floors and high ceilings, the kind of place that screamed professionalism and success.

Claire greeted him with a firm handshake and a welcoming smile. She was a tall woman with sharp features and a no-nonsense attitude that reminded Daniel of the businesspeople he used to work for back in the day. But there was kindness in her eyes, too, and a warmth that put him at ease.

"I've heard a lot about you from Angela," she said as they sat in her office, a spacious room with large windows overlooking the city. "She says you're the best at what you do."

Daniel shifted uncomfortably in his seat. He wasn't used to compliments anymore. "I've been out of the game for a while," he admitted, running a hand through his hair. "But I know how to run a cleaning crew. I built my business from the ground up once. I can do it again."

Claire nodded thoughtfully, tapping a pen against her desk. "That's what I like to hear. I'm willing to give you a chance, Daniel. Start small—just a few floors to begin with. If it works out, we'll expand the contract."

Daniel felt a surge of relief, his chest loosening for the first time in what felt like forever. "Thank you," he said, his voice thick with emotion. "You won't regret it."

When he returned home that evening, Angela was sitting on the couch, a sketchbook balanced on her lap, her face lit up with concentration as she worked on a design. The apartment was filled with the scent of fresh herbs and roasted vegetables—she had cooked dinner again, another thoughtful gesture that reminded Daniel just how much she cared. He stood in the doorway for a moment, watching her. She was in her element, her pencil flying across the paper, her brow furrowed in deep focus. This was the Angela he had known all those years ago— the artist, the dreamer. And yet, there was something different now. She wasn't just dreaming anymore; she was creating. And somehow, in the midst of his own mess, Daniel had become a part of that creation.

He cleared his throat, and Angela looked up, her face breaking into a smile when she saw him. "How did it go?" she asked, setting the sketchbook aside.

Daniel sat down beside her, the weight of the day still clinging to him, but this time it was a good kind of weight—the kind that came from moving forward. "It went well," he said, his voice steady. "I got the contract. It's small, but it's a start."

Angela's smile widened, her eyes bright with pride. "I knew you could do it."

For the first time in a long time, Daniel allowed himself to believe her. He let himself sink into the moment, into the warmth of the apartment, into the quiet joy that came from knowing that he was building something again. It wasn't just about the cleaning business, or the contracts, or even the money. It was about the fact that he was moving forward. He was starting over.

And Angela was there, right beside him.

The weeks passed, and as Daniel threw himself into his work, he found that the pieces of his old life started to fade into the background. The bitterness he had felt toward his ex-wife began to dull, replaced by a quiet acceptance. He had lost so much— his family, his home, his dignity. But here, in this small apartment with Angela, he was rebuilding. Every day, he went to work, cleaning office buildings with the same care and precision that had once made his business successful. And slowly, things started to grow. Angela was his biggest supporter. She was always there with words of encouragement, always there to remind him that he wasn't alone in this. She pushed him to keep going, even on the days when doubt crept back in, whispering that maybe this was all temporary, that maybe he would lose it all again. But Angela wouldn't let him give in to those thoughts. She believed in him—fully, completely.

And, in turn, Daniel found himself believing in her.

It wasn't just about his business anymore. Angela had her own dreams, her own ambitions. She had always been passionate about fashion, and now, with Daniel's encouragement, she started to take it more seriously. She worked late into the night, sketching designs, sewing fabric, and building a collection that reflected her own journey.

CHAPTER 5

As the weeks rolled by, Daniel and Angela's lives became intertwined in a way that felt natural, inevitable, as if they had always been meant to walk this path together. Their days were filled with work, but their nights became sacred—time reserved just for them. After long hours cleaning office buildings or sketching designs, they would sit together on the worn couch in Angela's living room, sharing stories about their days, planning, and dreaming about the future. One night, after dinner, Daniel sat on the floor with his back against the couch, the soft light from the lamp casting a warm glow over the room. Angela sat cross-legged beside him, her sketchbook balanced on her knees as she absentmindedly drew patterns in the margins of her designs. The air between them was quiet but filled with an unspoken energy, a kind of contentment that neither had felt in years.

"You know," Angela said, breaking the comfortable silence, "I've been thinking about expanding the collection. Maybe designing more than just clothes. I want to create something for plus-sized women that feels... empowering. Not just stylish, but like armor, you know?"

Daniel turned to look at her, intrigued by the sudden spark in her voice. He had seen her like this before, back in high school, when she'd talk endlessly about fashion, about how she wanted to change the way the world saw women like her—women with curves, with strength, with beauty that didn't fit into society's narrow boxes. Now, that same fire was back, and it was burning brighter than ever.

"What do you mean by armor?" Daniel asked, genuinely curious. He leaned back, propping himself up on his elbows, his eyes locked on her as she spoke.

Angela's eyes lit up, and she shifted excitedly in her seat. "I don't just want to make clothes that fit women like me," she explained, her hands moving animatedly as she spoke. "I want to create something that makes them feel powerful, confident. Like, when they put it on, they're ready to take on the world. You know, something that embraces who they are but doesn't try to hide it."

Daniel nodded, impressed by the passion behind her words. "That sounds incredible," he said, his voice low but full of admiration. "You've always had that vision, even back in high school. You never wanted to do things the traditional way."

Angela laughed softly, her cheeks flushing with a mix of pride and embarrassment. "Yeah, but back then, I didn't have the courage to actually pursue it. I was scared. Scared of failing, scared of what people would think."

"But you're not scared anymore," Daniel observed, his gaze steady. "You've come so far."

Angela met his eyes, and for a moment, the air between them grew still, heavy with the weight of unspoken understanding. "I'm not scared," she said quietly, her voice soft but resolute. "Not anymore. And a lot of that is because of you."

Daniel's heart skipped a beat at her words. He wasn't used to being someone's strength. For so long, he had been the one who needed saving, who needed support. But now, as Angela looked at him with such sincerity, he realized that he had become something more than just a man trying to rebuild his life. He had become her partner, her confidant, the person who believed in her even when she doubted herself. They fell into a comfortable silence again, the weight of their conversation settling around them like a warm blanket. Angela continued to sketch, her pencil moving across the page with the same steady determination that she applied to everything in her life. Daniel watched her for a while, his mind drifting to thoughts of the future—of what they could build together.

Angela wasn't the only one making strides in her career. Daniel's cleaning business was beginning to pick up momentum, slowly but surely. Claire had kept her word, and within a month, Daniel's contract had expanded to include more floors, more clients. It wasn't the empire he once had, but it was a start, and that was enough to keep him going. Daniel stood in the lobby of one of the office buildings he had just finished cleaning, wiping the sweat from his brow. The building was quiet now, the workday over, and the floors gleamed under the fluorescent lights. He looked around at the pristine surfaces, the sparkling windows, and felt a familiar sense of pride wash over him. This was his work—his hands had made this place shine. It wasn't glamorous, but it was honest, and that was all that mattered.

As he packed up his cleaning supplies, his phone buzzed in his pocket. He pulled it out and saw a message from Angela.

Got an exciting surprise for you. Meet me at the café down the street?

Daniel smiled to himself and typed a quick reply before heading out into the evening air. The city streets were bathed in the soft orange glow of the setting sun, and the scent of fresh bread from a nearby bakery filled the air. He walked briskly, his steps light as he made his way to the café.

When he arrived, Angela was already there, sitting at a small table near the window, her hands wrapped around a steaming mug of tea. She looked up when he entered, a wide smile spreading across her face.

"Hey, you," she greeted him warmly as he sat down across from her. "How was work?"

"Busy, but good," Daniel replied, settling into his seat. "What's the surprise?"

Angela's eyes twinkled with excitement as she reached into her bag and pulled out a small, neatly bound portfolio. She slid it across the table toward him, her fingers trembling slightly with anticipation. "I've been working on something, and I wanted you to be the first to see it."

Daniel raised an eyebrow and opened the portfolio. Inside were sketches—beautiful, intricate designs of clothing that seemed to leap off the page. Each piece was bold, confident, and unapologetically tailored for plus-sized women. He could see Angela's vision in every line, every curve. The clothes were more than just fabric—they were statements, declarations of self-worth and empowerment.

"These are amazing," Daniel breathed, his eyes scanning the pages. "Angela, you've outdone yourself."

Angela beamed, her pride palpable. "I've been working on this collection for months now, bit by bit. It's not finished yet, but I'm getting close. I'm calling it 'Empowered.' It's everything I've wanted to create—clothes that make women like me feel strong and beautiful."

Daniel looked up at her, his heart swelling with admiration. "You're going to change the world with this, you know that?"

Angela laughed, a blush creeping up her neck. "I don't know about that, but I'm hoping it'll at least make a difference for some women out there."

"It will," Daniel said with certainty. "I believe in you, Angela. I always have."

They sat in comfortable silence for a moment, the weight of their dreams hanging between them like a shared secret. For so long, both of them had been struggling—Angela with her fear of pursuing her passion, and Daniel with the wreckage of his old life. But now, sitting here together, it felt like they were finally on the cusp of something great. They weren't just surviving anymore. They were thriving.

The momentum continued to build over the next few months. Angela's designs started gaining traction online, with plus-sized influencers and bloggers taking notice of her bold, body-positive message. Orders started trickling in, and soon, she was spending every spare minute in her makeshift studio, sewing, designing, and planning for her next big move. Daniel, too, was growing. His cleaning business had expanded beyond Claire's office buildings, and he was now securing contracts with small businesses and high-end apartments. Every morning, he woke up with a renewed sense of purpose, knowing that he was building something real—something lasting. Angela stood beside him every step of the way, her faith in him unshakable. As summer turned to fall, the air outside took on a crispness that was both refreshing and invigorating. The streets of Weston Heights were lined with trees, their leaves shifting from green to fiery shades of orange and red. Daniel loved this time of year, the way the world felt alive with color and possibility. Each day, he found a little more of himself in the work he was doing—each office he cleaned, each floor he scrubbed felt like a step forward, not just for him but for Angela as well. One chilly evening, as they were winding down after a long day, Daniel found himself sprawled on the couch while Angela sat at the small dining table, surrounded by swaths of fabric and sketches. The living room was transformed into a makeshift studio, and Daniel marveled at how it seemed to reflect Angela's creativity and ambition. The soft hum of the sewing machine filled the air, punctuated by the occasional snip of scissors and Angela's focused murmurs as she talked herself through her designs.

"Daniel, can you come here for a second?" she called out, her voice cutting through his thoughts.

He pushed himself up and walked over, intrigued. "What's up?"

"I'm trying to decide on a fabric for the final piece in my collection," Angela explained, her brow furrowed in concentration as she held up two different materials. One was a deep burgundy velvet, rich and luxurious, while the other was a shimmering gold silk that caught the light beautifully. "What do you think? Should I go bold or elegant?"

Daniel looked at the fabrics, then at Angela, who was biting her lip in uncertainty. "I think both have their charm, but if you want it to make a statement, the velvet feels like it has more weight. It's powerful, just like your collection is meant to be."

Angela's face lit up, and she nodded enthusiastically. "You're right! The velvet it is!" She began to fold the gold silk away, her energy renewed. "I want this piece to be the centerpiece of the collection—the one that really embodies everything I'm trying to convey."

Daniel smiled as he watched her dive back into her work, her enthusiasm infectious. It was moments like this that reminded him of why they had come together; they complemented each other in ways neither had anticipated. She inspired him to work harder, to push through his doubts, while he gave her the confidence to embrace her dreams wholeheartedly.

4

However, as the weeks passed, not everything flowed smoothly. One evening, Daniel returned home to find Angela sitting at the dining table, her sketchbook closed in front of her, her expression distant. The room was filled with an unsettling silence, and he felt a tight knot forming in his stomach as he approached her.

"Hey, what's wrong?" he asked, pulling out a chair and sitting down beside her. "You look worried."

Angela sighed, running a hand through her hair, the weight of the world evident in her posture. "It's just... the collection is coming together, but I'm struggling to figure out how to market it. I want it to reach women who really need it, but I don't have the budget for advertising or a proper launch event."

Daniel leaned forward, concern etched on his face. "Have you thought about social media? You could use Instagram or TikTok to showcase your designs and reach out to influencers. I've seen people build whole businesses that way."

Angela nodded but looked skeptical. "I know, but I feel like it's a gamble. What if no one cares? What if I put myself out there and it flops? I don't want to disappoint anyone—especially you."

The vulnerability in her voice tugged at his heart. "You're not disappointing me, Angela. You're trying to do something incredible. It's okay to be scared; it's a part of the process. But you can't let fear hold you back. You've come so far already."

He could see the flicker of doubt in her eyes as she considered his words. "What if I put myself out there and get rejected? I've faced rejection before, and it hurt. I don't know if I can do it again."

"Angela, every successful person has faced rejection. It's part of the journey," Daniel urged, reaching across the table to take her hand. "You're passionate about this. You're talented. Remember how we talked about armor? This is your armor—

your chance to show the world what you can do. You can't let fear dictate your future."

She studied him for a moment, her expression softening as she absorbed his encouragement. "You really believe that?"

"Absolutely," he said with conviction. "You have something special to share. Just like you helped me find my footing, I know you can inspire others."

The tension in her shoulders eased as she squeezed his hand tightly, her resolve slowly rebuilding. "Okay, I'll think about it. Maybe I can start small, just post a few pictures and see what happens."

"That's the spirit!" Daniel grinned, his heart swelling with pride for her. They spent the rest of the evening brainstorming ideas, creating a plan for her social media presence. The air felt lighter now, filled with renewed hope and possibility.

CHAPTER 6

The following weeks brought about a flurry of activity as Angela immersed herself in creating content for her brand. She styled her clothes on a mannequin, capturing the vibrant colors and unique designs, and began taking photos around their apartment, using the natural light to showcase the textures and styles. With each post, she felt a surge of excitement, but also a pang of anxiety.

One afternoon, as they prepared for the weekend, Daniel watched as Angela set up her camera, adjusting the angle of her latest creation, the velvet dress that was meant to be the showstopper of her collection. The apartment was a whirlwind of fabric and ideas, and he couldn't help but feel proud of her determination.

"Just remember, it doesn't have to be perfect," he called from the kitchen, where he was chopping vegetables for dinner. "The most important thing is to be authentic. Your voice is what will resonate with people."

"Thanks, I appreciate that," she said, glancing over her shoulder with a grateful smile. "I'm just so nervous about how people will respond."

"Hey, you're a force," he reminded her gently. "You're creating something amazing. Trust in that."

As Angela began to model the dress, Daniel could see the spark reigniting within her. She moved with confidence, and the fabric flowed around her like a wave. With every click of the camera, he felt a sense of pride swelling within him—not just for her talent, but for the journey they were both on.

Later that night, after they had posted the photos online, they sat together, watching the notifications come in. A few likes trickled in, but Daniel could see the flicker of doubt returning to Angela's eyes. "What if this doesn't work?" she whispered, her voice barely audible over the soft hum of the evening.

"It will," Daniel replied firmly. "You've planted the seeds. Now it's time to let them grow. Just like my business, it takes time. We've both had our share of setbacks, but that doesn't mean we'll fail. It means we're learning."

Angela nodded, biting her lip as she stared at the screen, but there was a new determination in her eyes. "You're right. I just need to be patient.

Days turned into weeks, and soon Angela began to notice a shift. The photos she had posted started gaining traction, and comments flooded in with praise and encouragement. More importantly, she received messages from women who shared their own stories, expressing gratitude for her message of empowerment. As they were curled up on the couch, Daniel glanced over and noticed Angela's eyes sparkling with excitement. "You won't believe this!" she exclaimed, showing him her phone. "I just got a message from a well-known influencer who wants to collaborate! She loves the collection and wants to wear my designs!"

Daniel's heart raced as he read the message over her shoulder. "That's amazing, Angela! This could be your big break!"

The news sent a surge of energy through their apartment, and the atmosphere was electric with possibility. They spent the next few hours planning how to prepare for the collaboration—what pieces to showcase, how to style them, and what message they wanted to convey. With every idea they tossed around, Daniel felt the excitement growing, but he also noticed Angela's focus sharpening. She was in her element, driven by the fire of opportunity. As the collaboration date approached, the apartment became a hive of creativity. Angela worked tirelessly, often late into the night, sewing and tweaking each design, ensuring they reflected the powerful message she wanted to convey. Daniel was her unwavering support, lifting her spirits when fatigue set in and helping her prepare for the influencer's arrival. Finally, the day arrived for the influencer's visit. The air was thick with anticipation, and Angela was a bundle of nerves, her fingers fidgeting as she paced around their small living room. Daniel could see the worry etched across her face, so he stepped in to soothe her anxiety.

"You've got this, Angela. Remember, you've worked hard for this moment," he said, his voice calm and steady. "Just be yourself and let your passion shine."

With a deep breath, she nodded, and together they set up the living room, turning it into a mini runway. Daniel helped rearrange furniture, draping fabric over chairs to create a backdrop that showcased Angela's designs. They worked in perfect harmony, their movements flowing together like a well-rehearsed dance.

When the influencer finally arrived, Daniel could sense the tension in the air. But as Angela greeted her with warmth and authenticity, he saw her confidence return. They talked and laughed, Angela explaining her vision behind each piece and how they were designed to empower women. Daniel stood back, a quiet pride swelling in his chest as he watched the two women connect. The influencer slipped into the velvet dress, and Daniel felt a rush of excitement as she stepped out to show them. The fabric hugged her curves perfectly, the rich color contrasting beautifully against her skin. Angela's eyes lit up as she took in the sight, her dream coming to life right before her eyes.

"This is stunning," the influencer exclaimed, twirling to admire the design. "I can feel the strength in this piece. I'm honored to wear it."

As the shoot progressed, Daniel felt a sense of peace enveloping him. He could see the joy radiating from Angela as she engaged with her muse, and it was clear that the moment was transforming her. She was no longer just a woman trying to find her way; she was an artist, a creator, and an advocate for the women she sought to empower.

After the influencer left, the apartment buzzed with excitement. The photoshoot had gone better than they had hoped, and Angela's heart soared with the possibilities that lay ahead. That night, they celebrated with a simple dinner—pasta and salad—enjoying the warmth of each other's company.

"Do you think this is really going to change things?" Angela asked, her eyes sparkling with hope as they clinked their glasses together.

"I know it will," Daniel replied, his voice steady and reassuring. "You've poured your heart into this. It's going to resonate with women out there."

As they sat together, the flickering candlelight casting shadows on the walls, Daniel felt a surge of gratitude for the journey they had embarked on together. They were two people who had faced their demons and emerged stronger, not just as individuals but as partners. Angela's dream was blossoming, and he felt blessed to be a part of it.

Over the next few weeks, as orders began to roll in and her social media following grew, Angela's designs took off. Each new order represented not just a sale, but a woman's story, a woman embracing her body and feeling empowered in her own skin. Daniel could hardly contain his pride as he watched her flourish.

With each success, they celebrated together, each milestone bringing them closer. Their relationship deepened, the love they shared transforming into something solid and steadfast. Angela inspired him, and he became her rock, and together, they built a life filled with purpose.

As their lives continued to intertwine, Daniel and Angela faced challenges, triumphs, and moments of doubt, but through it all, they remained committed to each other. With every step they took, they reaffirmed their belief in the power of love, resilience, and the unwavering spirit that had brought them together in the first place. As winter approached, the first snowfall dusted the streets of Weston Heights, transforming the town into a picturesque winter wonderland. The chilly air filled with the scent of pine and cinnamon, and holiday decorations twinkled along storefronts, adding a festive glow to the surroundings. Daniel and Angela took advantage of the holiday spirit, venturing out to explore local markets, soaking in the joy and warmth that radiated from the community.

After a time had passed, they found themselves at a quaint little café that had become a staple in their neighborhood. The cozy interior, adorned with soft lighting and rustic wooden furniture, provided a warm haven from the biting cold outside. As they settled into a booth, Daniel took a moment to observe Angela, who was animatedly discussing her plans for the upcoming fashion show that would showcase her collection.

"I can't believe I'm actually doing this!" Angela exclaimed, her eyes sparkling with excitement. "The event is going to be huge, and I'm so grateful for the support we've received. I never imagined it would come together like this."

Daniel reached across the table, taking her hand in his. "You deserve every bit of this success, Angela. You've worked so hard, and your passion is contagious. I can't wait to see everything come to life."

Angela squeezed his hand, her expression softening. "I couldn't have done it without you. You've been my rock through all of this. I don't know where I'd be if you hadn't believed in me."

With the holiday season in full swing, they decided to host a small gathering for friends and family. Daniel envisioned a cozy evening filled with laughter, good food, and celebration—a way to honor the progress they had made together. As they prepared for the party, the atmosphere in their apartment became electric with anticipation.

They spent days decorating, stringing lights across the ceiling, and creating a festive vibe that felt both warm and inviting. Angela baked cookies while Daniel cooked up a feast, their laughter filling the space as they playfully tossed flour at each other and danced around the kitchen.

The night of the gathering arrived, and the apartment buzzed with life as friends and family filtered in. Daniel stood at the door, welcoming guests with a warm smile, while Angela flitted about, ensuring everyone felt at home. The room was filled with the aroma of delicious food and the sounds of cheerful chatter, and Daniel felt a sense of belonging wash over him. As he mingled, he caught sight of Angela across the room, her laughter ringing out like music as she engaged with a group of friends. She looked radiant, her smile lighting up her face, and he felt a rush of gratitude for how far they had come together.

At one point, Angela made her way over to him, her cheeks flushed with happiness. "Can you believe how many people showed up? It's amazing!" She beamed, her eyes sparkling.

"It really is," Daniel replied, pulling her close for a brief hug. "I'm so proud of you, and I can feel how much this means to you."

As the night wore on, Daniel took a moment to reflect on the journey that had led them to this point. He thought of the dark days of homelessness, the uncertainty of their futures, and the sheer willpower it took to rise from those depths. He had never imagined that a chance encounter with his old high school girlfriend would lead to this—standing here, surrounded by friends, love, and a sense of hope.

When the time came to make a toast, Daniel stood before the gathered crowd, raising his glass high. "To friendship, love, and new beginnings," he proclaimed, his voice strong and steady. "We've all faced challenges, but tonight, we celebrate not just our victories, but the connections that lift us up and carry us forward. Here's to Angela, for being a beacon of hope and inspiration for all of us."

Cheers erupted around the room, and Angela's eyes glistened with gratitude as she looked at him. In that moment, Daniel felt the weight of their shared experiences and the strength of their bond—a bond forged in adversity and tempered by love. As the new year rolled in, Daniel and Angela found themselves setting goals together, both personally and professionally. They spent evenings discussing dreams, aspirations, and what the future held for them as a couple. They wanted to build not just a business but a life that resonated with their values and ambitions.

Angela had decided to take her business to the next level by expanding her collection to include accessories and home décor. "I want to create a lifestyle brand that empowers women, not just through clothing but through every aspect of their lives," she explained, her voice filled with determination. "I want to help them feel beautiful and confident in every way."

Daniel was inspired by her vision. "I love that idea! You have the talent and passion to make it happen. We can work together to build the brand and reach even more people."

As winter faded into spring, they invested their energy into launching the new collection. Angela poured her heart into the designs, while Daniel applied his business acumen to marketing strategies, networking, and building partnerships with local businesses.

One Saturday, they attended a local artisan market, showcasing Angela's designs for the first time. The sun shone brightly, and the atmosphere was vibrant with the sounds of laughter and music. As they set up their booth, Daniel could feel the excitement buzzing around them.

"This is it!" Angela said, her voice laced with exhilaration as she arranged the clothing on display. "I can't believe we're finally doing this."

Daniel smiled, feeling a swell of pride. "Just remember, no matter what happens today, we've already accomplished so much together."

As the day progressed, they interacted with potential customers, sharing stories about their journey and the inspiration behind Angela's designs. The response was overwhelmingly positive, and as the sun began to set, they tallied up their sales with astonished smiles.

"I can't believe we did it!" Angela exclaimed, her eyes wide with disbelief. "This is just the beginning!"

4

However, just as things seemed to be going smoothly, the challenges they faced began to mount. Angela's ambition and success attracted attention, but not all of it was positive. Criticism and self-doubt crept in, fueled by whispers of competition and insecurities.

One evening, as they sat together on the couch, Angela opened up about her feelings. "I can't shake this nagging doubt. What if I'm not good enough? What if people start comparing me to other designers? I just don't know if I can handle the pressure."

Daniel could see the turmoil within her, the fears that threatened to overshadow her confidence. He reached for her hand, drawing her attention. "You are more than good enough. You've worked hard to create something beautiful, and you're inspiring so many people. Don't let anyone else's opinions define your worth."

"But what if it all falls apart?" Angela whispered, her voice trembling. "What if I can't keep up with the expectations?"

"Then we'll face it together," he reassured her, his gaze steady. "Remember what we talked about—growth comes from challenges. You don't have to do this alone. I'm right here, every step of the way."

She nodded slowly, taking in his words. "You're right. I can't give in to fear. I need to remember why I started this in the first place."

Daniel watched as she took a deep breath, her resolve slowly returning. "Exactly. Your journey is just beginning, and I believe in you."

The culmination of their hard work came to fruition when Angela was invited to showcase her collection at a major fashion show. The opportunity was a dream come true, and the pressure was intense. The days leading up to the event were filled with late nights, fittings, and final touches, but Daniel remained by her side, providing unwavering support. On the night of the show, the atmosphere was electric. The venue was adorned with elegant decorations, and the runway was lit with bright lights that glimmered like stars. As Angela prepared backstage, her heart raced with anticipation and anxiety.

"You look stunning," Daniel said as he helped her with the final adjustments to her outfit, his voice low and reassuring.

"Thanks," she replied, her voice trembling with nerves. "I just hope I can pull this off."

"You will," he assured her. "Just focus on what you've worked so hard for. This is your moment."

When it was time for her to take the stage, Daniel felt a mix of pride and anxiety. He watched as she stepped out onto the runway, her designs shining in the spotlight. The audience's applause was thunderous, and he felt a swell of emotion as he cheered her on, knowing how much this moment meant to her.

With each step she took, Angela exuded confidence, her passion radiating through her designs. As she posed for the cameras, Daniel saw the transformation that had taken place within her—a woman who had once struggled with self-doubt was now a powerful force, commanding attention and respect.

questioning whether she could sustain the level of success they had achieved. There were days when the weight of it all seemed overwhelming.

"Daniel, what if this is just a fluke?" Angela confided one evening after a particularly stressful day.

Daniel turned from the sink where he was washing dishes and faced Angela, her words thick with doubt. She sat at the kitchen island, her eyes distant, her fingers absentmindedly tracing the grain of the wood. He could see the exhaustion etched in her features, the weight of the pressure hanging heavily over her like a storm cloud.

He dried his hands with a towel, walked over, and gently placed his hands on her shoulders. "It's not a fluke, Angela," he said softly, his voice steady with conviction. "You've built something real, something lasting. But you're human. It's okay to feel overwhelmed."

She sighed, looking up at him, her eyes filled with uncertainty. "I didn't think it would be like this," she admitted. "I thought once I made it, I'd feel secure. But the higher I climb, the more I worry about falling."

Daniel knelt beside her, leveling his gaze with hers. "I get it. Success is terrifying because you care so much about it. That fear is part of the process. But you can't let it paralyze you. You've faced much worse, and you've come out stronger every single time."

Angela's eyes softened, but the tension in her body remained. "I just don't want to disappoint anyone. I don't want to lose everything we've worked for."

He took her hand, his fingers interlacing with hers. "You won't lose it. We won't. And even if things change, we adapt. You're not in this alone. We'll face whatever comes together."

For a moment, she was silent, her breathing slow and steady as she absorbed his words. There was something reassuring about Daniel's presence. He had always been a source of calm amid her chaos, a reminder that she didn't have to carry the world on her shoulders alone.

"I don't know what I'd do without you," she whispered, her voice thick with emotion.

Daniel smiled, brushing a strand of hair behind her ear. "Good thing you'll never have to find out."

Angela let out a soft laugh, the weight of her worries momentarily lifting. It was in these small moments, these quiet affirmations of love and partnership, that she found her strength again.

CHAPTER 7

As the weeks went on, Angela took Daniel's words to heart. She began to prioritize her well-being, finding balance between the demands of her growing business and the need for self-care. She learned to set boundaries, to delegate responsibilities, and to trust in the team she had built around her. But success also brought unexpected opportunities. One afternoon, while Angela was reviewing fabric samples in her studio, her phone buzzed with a call. She glanced at the screen, her eyebrows raising in surprise when she saw the name of a major retailer on the caller ID. Heart pounding, she answered the call and was greeted by a representative who expressed interest in carrying her line in select stores across the country. The offer was huge, a potential game-changer for her brand, but it also meant scaling up quickly—something that both excited and terrified her.

After the call ended, Angela paced the length of her studio, her mind racing with possibilities and concerns. She knew this opportunity could propel her business to new heights, but it also meant taking on a level of risk she hadn't yet faced.

When Daniel came home that evening, he found her deep in thought, her expression a mixture of excitement and apprehension.

"I just got a call from [major retailer]," she said, looking up at him with wide eyes. "They want to carry my line in their stores."

Daniel's face lit up with pride, but he could sense her hesitation. "That's incredible, Angela! This is huge!"

"I know," she said, her voice a little shaky. "But… it's also terrifying. If I agree, I'll have to expand production, hire more people, deal with distribution… It's a lot. And if it doesn't work out, it could set us back in ways I'm not sure I'm ready for."

He stepped closer, his hand resting on her back. "You don't have to decide right away. Take some time to weigh the pros and cons. But remember, you've been handling challenges like this from the start. You've built this business from the ground up, and you can handle whatever comes next."

Angela nodded, her gaze distant as she processed the enormity of the opportunity. "It just feels like a tipping point, you know? Like whatever decision I make here will change everything."

Daniel smiled, his voice calm and steady. "That's the nature of growth, isn't it? Every step forward feels risky because it's new. But that's where the magic happens. You've got this, Angela. And no matter what happens, I'm here for you."

While Angela wrestled with the pressures of her burgeoning success, Daniel found himself confronted with unresolved issues from his past. One afternoon, while he was at his cleaning company's office, he received an unexpected phone call that threw him off balance. It was from his ex-wife, Sarah—the woman who had left him during his lowest point. Hearing her voice on the other end of the line after so many years sent a wave of conflicting emotions through him. The bitterness, hurt, and betrayal he had buried came rushing back, but there was also a sense of detachment. He had rebuilt his life without her, had found love again with Angela, and yet, the call dredged up memories he had long since tried to forget.

"Daniel… I didn't know how else to reach you," Sarah said hesitantly. "I've been thinking a lot about everything, and I wanted to apologize. For leaving, for everything I did to you."

There was a long pause as Daniel processed her words. He had never expected an apology, never thought she would look back and regret her actions. "It was a long time ago, Sarah," he said carefully, his voice measured. "I've moved on. We both have."

"I know," she said quietly. "But I just… I needed to say it. I was wrong to leave you like that, especially when you were going through so much. I wasn't strong enough to handle it, and I took the easy way out. I've regretted it ever since."

The sincerity in her voice caught him off guard. He could hear the weight of her guilt, the regret that had been festering for years. But as she spoke, Daniel realized something. He no longer carried the same anger or hurt. He had found healing in his journey with Angela, in rebuilding his life from the ground up. He didn't need closure from Sarah because he had already made peace with it on his own.

"I appreciate the apology," Daniel said finally, his tone calm and even. "But I've moved past it. I hope you've found what you were looking for, too."

There was another pause, then Sarah responded softly, "I'm glad you're doing well, Daniel. I really am. I just wanted you to know that I'm sorry."

When the call ended, Daniel sat in silence for a long moment. He stared out the window, watching the world move on without the weight of his past dragging him down. He realized that, in the end, it wasn't Sarah's apology that mattered—it was the life he had built after her, the love he had found in Angela, and the strength he had discovered within himself.

That evening, Daniel told Angela about the call from Sarah. They sat together in the living room, the soft glow of the fireplace casting flickering shadows on the walls.

"How do you feel about it?" Angela asked, her voice gentle, as she took his hand.

Daniel thought for a moment, then smiled. "Free, I guess. For a long time, I didn't realize how much her leaving affected me. But I don't need her to make things right anymore. I've already done that for myself."

Angela squeezed his hand, a soft smile spreading across her face. "I'm proud of you. It takes a lot of strength to let go of that kind of hurt."

They sat in comfortable silence for a moment, the quiet intimacy of the room wrapping around them like a blanket. Daniel looked at her, feeling the profound sense of peace that had settled into his life since they had come together.

"You know," he said softly, "I wouldn't trade any of it. The hardships, the heartbreak. It all led me to you."

Angela's eyes shone with emotion, and she leaned in to kiss him gently. "And I wouldn't trade you for the world."

As they sat together, watching the fire crackle and dance, they knew that whatever challenges lay ahead, they would face them side by side—stronger, wiser, and more connected than ever before. Together, they had weathered storms and built a life out of love, resilience, and faith. Angela sat in the plush leather chair at the head of her office's conference room table, the soft murmur of the city barely audible through the thick, tinted glass windows that framed the skyline. It was early evening, the golden light of the setting sun reflecting off the high-rise buildings that filled her view. The downtown vista stretched out before her, a constant reminder of everything she had built and the world she now occupied—a far cry from where she had started. The room was silent except for the faint ticking of the clock, and in front of her lay the contract that could redefine everything she had worked for. The thick stack of papers represented years of sacrifice—late nights hunched over fabric samples, weekends spent sketching designs instead of enjoying her life, the constant balancing act between creativity and survival. Her brand had grown from a fledgling idea into a force that now had the attention of one of the largest department store chains in the country. This contract was the culmination of all of it. If she signed, it would catapult her business into a national spotlight, cementing her position in an industry that wasn't kind to newcomers, let alone those who built their empire from nothing.

Angela leaned back slightly, her eyes tracing the lines of the text on the contract. The legal jargon, though explained by her team of attorneys, still felt dense, cold, and detached from the passion that had fueled her journey. Her fingers drummed lightly against the table, her mind racing, each beat of her heart pounding with the weight of the decision before her. She had always been confident—strong-willed, focused, and determined to carve out her space in the world. Yet, in this moment, there was a knot of uncertainty lodged in her chest. This was the dream she had fought for, but now, staring at the contract, the enormity of it all felt suffocating. It was a crossroads. Signing this document meant stepping into a realm of corporate partnerships and demands that could pull her creative vision in directions she hadn't anticipated. Angela pushed her chair back slightly, the leather creaking beneath her, and stood up, walking toward the floor-to-ceiling windows that offered a panoramic view of the city. She placed her hand against the cool glass, looking down at the streets below where people hurried through their routines, oblivious to the weight of the decision she was making several stories above. For years, she had fought to stay true to her vision, resisting offers that felt like they would compromise her brand. But this contract was different. It was a game-changer. She closed her eyes for a moment, thinking back to the early days—working out of her spare bedroom, pushing through exhaustion, and wondering if any of it would ever amount to anything more than a dream. Those years felt distant now, almost like someone else's life. But with them came the memory of freedom, of creating without pressure or expectation. This contract, while offering the world, also threatened to take some of that away.

Angela sighed, opening her eyes again, her gaze drifting back to the contract on the table. The city outside was still bathed in that golden light, the day slipping into evening. She had made it this far on her own terms, and now, standing at the edge of something bigger than she had ever imagined, she couldn't help but wonder if she could continue to do so. The clock ticked on, but Angela remained still, weighing the gravity of her decision in the silence of the room. Angela felt the warmth of Daniel's body against her own as she stood by the window, gazing out over the city that had both lifted her up and pressed her down. She didn't move right away, instead allowing herself to sink into the quiet comfort of his presence. His arm around her waist felt like an anchor, a tether to something real, something that wasn't tied to contracts, deadlines, or the constant push for more. For a few moments, neither of them spoke. The hum of the city below filled the silence, a distant reminder that the world was still turning outside of the conference room. But here, in this small, fleeting moment, it was just the two of them, wrapped in a shared understanding that didn't need words.

Daniel broke the silence first, his voice low and steady. "It's a lot, isn't it?" He didn't need to ask what was weighing on her mind—he had seen the tension in her shoulders, the way her expression had hardened as the pressure mounted. He knew her better than anyone, and he could sense when she was carrying more than she let on.

Angela nodded, her forehead resting against the cool glass. "Sometimes I wonder if it's worth it," she admitted, her voice barely above a whisper. She hadn't said those words aloud before—not to him, not to anyone. But at this moment, with Daniel standing beside her, she didn't have to pretend.

Daniel didn't respond right away. Instead, he tightened his grip around her waist, his hand sliding up to rest gently on her back. It wasn't reassurance she needed—Angela was too strong for empty words. What she needed was the space to say what was on her mind without judgment, and he understood that.

"You've built something incredible," he said after a moment, his voice soft but firm. "But it's okay to question it. It's okay to wonder if the cost is too high."

Angela exhaled slowly, her breath fogging the glass in front of her. "It feels like I've been running so hard for so long, and now that I'm here..." She trailed off, unsure of how to finish the thought. The truth was, now that she was here—at the brink of the success she had always dreamed of—it didn't feel the way she thought it would. There was no relief, no sense of triumph. Just more pressure, more decisions that felt like they had the weight of the world behind them.

Daniel turned her gently so she was facing him, his hands resting on her arms. He looked down at her with a seriousness that matched the gravity of her feelings. "You don't have to do this alone, Ang. You don't have to carry all of this by yourself." His voice was steady, the same way it had been the first time he told her he was staying—through everything, no matter what.

Angela looked up at him, her eyes searching his face for the reassurance she hadn't realized she needed. She had always been independent, always driven by her own ambition, but in Daniel, she had found someone who didn't want to take away her strength, but instead, stood beside her, offering a quiet, unwavering support.

"I know," she said finally, her voice softening. "It's just... a lot."

Daniel nodded, understanding without needing to press further. "Then let's figure it out, together," he said simply, his thumb gently brushing against her arm.

For the first time in what felt like weeks, Angela allowed herself to relax. She didn't have to make the decision right now. She didn't have to carry the weight of it all in this moment. The future could wait—just for a little while.

"Thank you," she whispered, resting her head against his chest, listening to the steady beat of his heart.

Daniel pressed a kiss to the top of her head, holding her close. "We'll get through it," he said quietly, and in his voice, Angela found the reassurance she needed. It wasn't a solution, and it didn't erase the pressures she faced, but it was enough. Enough for now.

Daniel's hands moved from her shoulders to her arms, squeezing gently as if to anchor her in the moment. "I know it feels like that right now," he said quietly, his voice steady. "But you're not just staying afloat—you're steering the ship. You've been doing it this whole time, even when you didn't realize it. When things got tough, you pushed through. And when everyone doubted you, you kept going." He paused, letting the weight of his words sink in. "You're not just surviving, Angela. You're thriving."

She lowered her gaze, her thoughts still churning despite his steady encouragement. It was hard for her to see what he saw. All she felt was the pressure mounting day by day, the weight of expectations, the constant fear of failure creeping up behind her. She had worked too hard to lose it all now, and that fear—of letting everything slip through her fingers—clung to her more tightly than she liked to admit.

"I don't know how to stop thinking about it," she said softly, her voice carrying the vulnerability she rarely let anyone hear. "The what-ifs keep me up at night."

Daniel tilted her chin up gently so she could meet his gaze. His eyes were calm, reassuring, filled with a certainty she wished she could borrow for herself. "The what-ifs will always be there," he said, "but they don't get to decide how this turns out. You do. You've already made it through more than most people ever will. This isn't something you're just going to lose control of—it's yours. And if it gets hard, you've got me. You're not doing this alone."

Angela's lips twitched into a small smile, a flicker of relief breaking through her worry. "You always know what to say," she murmured, leaning into him again, the tension in her body slowly unwinding as she rested against his chest.

Daniel wrapped his arms around her, holding her close. "That's because I believe in you," he said simply. "Even when you don't believe in yourself."

They stood there in silence for a while, the weight of the city beyond the window feeling distant, almost insignificant for just a moment. Angela let herself absorb his words, feeling the strength in them, the truth she couldn't quite bring herself to see but knew was there.

And in that quiet, with Daniel's arms around her and the city buzzing far below, Angela felt something shift inside her—a small but significant release of the fear she had been clinging to. It wasn't gone, not completely, but it felt more manageable now. The doubts would return, she knew that. But with Daniel by her side, the weight didn't feel quite as unbearable.

Angela's expression softened, her grip on Daniel's hand tightening slightly as she absorbed his words. "You make it sound so simple," she said, a faint smile tugging at her lips. "Like everything's going to be okay just because you're here."

Daniel chuckled softly, his thumb brushing over the back of her hand in small circles. "It's not simple. None of this is. But it's easier when you're not facing it alone. You've been carrying all of this weight by yourself for so long, Ang. You don't have to anymore."

She exhaled slowly, the tension in her shoulders easing just a little. "It's hard to let go of that, though. I've always been the one to handle things, to fix them."

"I know," Daniel said, his voice quiet but firm. "But you don't have to fix everything by yourself. Not anymore."

They stood there for a moment, the silence between them comfortable, the weight of their conversation settling in. Angela's mind raced with thoughts of contracts, deadlines, and all the things that could still go wrong. But for the first time in a long time, she didn't feel quite so overwhelmed by it all. Daniel's presence, his unwavering support, was enough to calm the storm inside her, even if only for a while.

"I'm scared," she admitted, her voice barely above a whisper. "Of failing. Of losing everything I've worked for."

Daniel met her gaze, his expression serious. "It's okay to be scared. But don't let that fear stop you from moving forward. You've come too far to let doubt hold you back now."

Angela nodded slowly, her fingers still intertwined with his. She didn't have all the answers, and she knew the fear would never completely go away. But standing here, with Daniel by her side, she felt a little more certain that, whatever came next, she could face it. Not alone, but together.

"Thank you," she whispered, her voice laced with gratitude. "For always being there."

Daniel smiled, pressing a gentle kiss to her forehead. "Always," he said softly, pulling her into a warm embrace, holding her tight as if to remind her she wasn't alone in this, not anymore. The next morning, the air in Angela's office seemed heavier, thick with anticipation. She had arrived early, before the usual bustle of her team, and the soft hum of the city beyond the windows seemed distant, muffled in the quiet stillness. The contract sat on her desk, an unassuming stack of papers that carried the weight of her future. She stared at it, feeling the gravity of the moment settle on her shoulders—just like it had so many times before. But today, the weight felt different, somehow less overwhelming, more within her control.

Taking a deep breath, Angela reached out and ran her fingers along the edge of the paper, its surface cool and crisp under her fingertips. This was it—the culmination of years of dedication, the countless sleepless nights, the relentless push through doubt and exhaustion. Every dream, every sacrifice she'd made, had brought her to this point. Her heart thudded against her ribcage, the adrenaline mixing with fear, with hope, with the sharp edge of possibility. The pen in her hand felt light but significant as she hovered over the signature line. For a moment, she hesitated. She closed her eyes and let the memories flood in—the long hours spent bent over her sewing machine, fingers numb from pinning fabric, the late nights sketching designs only to tear them up in frustration, the tiny triumphs that had kept her going, inching her closer to this very moment. Each struggle had shaped her, and now here she was, on the brink of turning it all into something real, something lasting.

With a deep breath and a steady hand, Angela pressed the pen to the paper. Her name flowed across the page, the ink bleeding into the fibers, stark and irrevocable. The second the pen lifted from the paper, a wave of calm washed over her. It was done. A finality settled in, but instead of fear, there was peace. She had made the choice, and now all that remained was to move forward.

The contract was signed, and with it, a new chapter had begun.

Later that evening, Angela and Daniel sat together in the heart of their home—the small, intimate living room that had become a sanctuary for both of them. A bottle of champagne chilled in the fridge, its glass surface slick with condensation, waiting for the right moment to be opened. The room itself, though modest in size, felt rich with warmth, a kind of lived-in coziness that only years of shared memories could bring. The soft glow of the table lamp cast a golden light across the space, bathing everything in a warm, honeyed hue that made the entire room feel like it was wrapped in a comforting embrace.

The walls were lined with framed sketches, Angela's earliest designs etched in graphite and ink, each one a testament to her relentless pursuit of her dreams. Some were rough, hastily drawn ideas captured in fleeting moments of inspiration, while others were polished, fully realized concepts, each a stepping stone on her path toward something bigger. Each frame held not just a piece of her work, but a fragment of her journey—a journey that had seen its share of struggles, doubts, and small triumphs along the way. The room was alive with those memories, as if the very air hummed with the energy of everything she had worked for. Daniel sat beside her on the familiar, well-worn couch, a small glass of champagne already cradled in his hands. The couch itself, though frayed at the edges and sagging in all the places they sat most often, had long ago molded itself to fit them perfectly. It was more than just furniture; it was a silent witness to late-night conversations, quiet moments of comfort, and shared laughter. Daniel's fingers traced the rim of his glass absentmindedly as he gazed at her, his eyes filled with a kind of quiet pride that didn't need words to be understood.

Raising his glass, Daniel smiled at her, his expression soft but filled with meaning. "To big risks," he said, his voice warm and sincere, the weight of the day slowly fading from his tone. "And even bigger rewards."

Angela's lips curled into a smile, her laughter a soft, musical sound that filled the room, as if the very walls leaned in to listen. She lifted her glass to meet his, the delicate *clink* of crystal echoing in the space between them, sealing the moment with an unspoken promise. "To us," she replied, her voice carrying the weight of everything they had been through together—every hardship, every moment of doubt, and every quiet victory they had celebrated side by side.

They both sipped from their glasses, the cool champagne a refreshing contrast to the warm atmosphere around them. The bubbles danced across her tongue, light and effervescent, a fleeting but joyful sensation that mirrored how she felt in that moment. For a while, they sat in silence, letting the world outside their cozy little room fade away, the day's burdens slowly melting in the presence of each other.

Angela's gaze drifted around the room, taking in the familiar sights with a newfound appreciation. There was something about this moment that made everything seem more vivid, more meaningful. The worn couch, with its faded cushions and threadbare arms, wasn't just a piece of furniture—it was a symbol of their resilience. The stack of fashion magazines on the coffee table, some of their covers dog-eared and worn from constant use, represented her endless drive for inspiration, her hunger to create something beautiful. And there, on the far wall, hung the framed photograph of the two of them from their high school days—young and smiling, captured in a moment when their lives had seemed full of endless possibilities. Back then, the future had been an abstract concept, something distant and undefined. Now, it felt tangible, like something they had fought for and earned together.

"It feels real now," Angela murmured after a long pause, her voice barely above a whisper as she set her glass down on the coffee table. The sound of the glass meeting wood was soft, almost imperceptible, but it felt like a defining moment in the quiet stillness of the room. "The contract, the expansion... it's actually happening."

Daniel, who had been watching her with quiet intensity, nodded slowly, his hand finding its way to hers. He shifted closer, the familiar scent of him—clean soap, a hint of aftershave—comforting in its familiarity. His arm draped over her shoulder, pulling her into his warmth, as if he could shield her from the weight of the world outside their walls. "It's been happening, Ang," he said softly, his voice steady and sure. "You've been building this for years. The contract... it's just the next chapter."

She leaned into him, her body relaxing against his as if it had always been meant to be there, perfectly aligned with his. She could hear his heartbeat, a steady, rhythmic thrum beneath her cheek, and it anchored her, grounding her in the moment. The weight of the day, of the decision she had made, seemed to lift slightly as she let herself simply be—be present, be here with him, be hopeful for what lay ahead.

"I couldn't have done it without you," she whispered, the words heavy with truth. It wasn't just gratitude that filled her voice; it was a deep, unshakable knowledge that Daniel had been her rock, her steady hand guiding her through the stormy seas of uncertainty. Without him, she wasn't sure she would have had the strength to see it through.

Daniel smiled, a soft, almost imperceptible curve of his lips, and pressed a gentle kiss to the top of her head. "And I wouldn't have wanted to do anything else," he murmured, his breath warm against her hair.

In that moment, surrounded by the quiet hum of their shared space, everything seemed to align. The future, once a daunting unknown, now felt like something they could face together, one step at a time. The challenges that lay ahead no longer seemed insurmountable. They had each other. They had come this far. And now, they were ready for whatever came next.

That evening, Angela and Daniel sat together in the heart of their home—the small, intimate living room that had become a sanctuary for both of them. A bottle of champagne chilled in the fridge, its glass surface slick with condensation, waiting for the right moment to be opened. The room itself, though modest in size, felt rich with warmth, a kind of lived-in coziness that only years of shared memories could bring. The soft glow of the table lamp cast a golden light across the space, bathing everything in a warm, honeyed hue that made the entire room feel like it was wrapped in a comforting embrace. The walls were lined with framed sketches, Angela's earliest designs etched in graphite and ink, each one a testament to her relentless pursuit of her dreams. Some were rough, hastily drawn ideas captured in fleeting moments of inspiration, while others were polished, fully realized concepts, each a stepping stone on her path toward something bigger. Each frame held not just a piece of her work, but a fragment of her journey—a journey that had seen its share of struggles, doubts, and small triumphs along the way. The room was alive with those memories, as if the very air hummed with the energy of everything she had worked for. Daniel sat beside her on the familiar, well-worn couch, a small glass of champagne already cradled in his hands. The couch itself, though frayed at the edges and sagging in all the places they sat most often, had long ago molded itself to fit them perfectly. It was more than just furniture; it was a silent witness to late-night conversations, quiet moments of comfort, and shared laughter. Daniel's fingers traced the rim of his glass absentmindedly as he gazed at her, his eyes filled with a kind of quiet pride that didn't need words to be understood.

Raising his glass, Daniel smiled at her, his expression soft but filled with meaning. "To big risks," he said, his voice warm and sincere, the weight of the day slowly fading from his tone. "And even bigger rewards."

Angela's lips curled into a smile, her laughter a soft, musical sound that filled the room, as if the very walls leaned in to listen. She lifted her glass to meet his, the delicate *clink* of crystal echoing in the space between them, sealing the moment with an unspoken promise. "To us," she replied, her voice carrying the weight of everything they had been through together—every hardship, every moment of doubt, and every quiet victory they had celebrated side by side.

They both sipped from their glasses, the cool champagne a refreshing contrast to the warm atmosphere around them. The bubbles danced across her tongue, light and effervescent, a fleeting but joyful sensation that mirrored how she felt in that moment. For a while, they sat in silence, letting the world outside their cozy little room fade away, the day's burdens slowly melting in the presence of each other.

Angela's gaze drifted around the room, taking in the familiar sights with a newfound appreciation. There was something about this moment that made everything seem more vivid, more meaningful. The worn couch, with its faded cushions and threadbare arms, wasn't just a piece of furniture—it was a symbol of their resilience. The stack of fashion magazines on the coffee table, some of their covers dog-eared and worn from constant use, represented her endless drive for inspiration, her hunger to create something beautiful. And there, on the far wall, hung the framed photograph of the two of them from their high school days—young and smiling, captured in a moment when their lives had seemed full of endless possibilities. Back then, the future had been an abstract concept, something distant and undefined. Now, it felt tangible, like something they had fought for and earned together.

"It feels real now," Angela murmured after a long pause, her voice barely above a whisper as she set her glass down on the coffee table. The sound of the glass meeting wood was soft, almost imperceptible, but it felt like a defining moment in the quiet stillness of the room. "The contract, the expansion... it's actually happening."

Daniel, who had been watching her with quiet intensity, nodded slowly, his hand finding its way to hers. He shifted closer, the familiar scent of him—clean soap, a hint of aftershave—comforting in its familiarity. His arm draped over her shoulder, pulling her into his warmth, as if he could shield her from the weight of the world outside their walls. "It's been happening, Ang," he said softly, his voice steady and sure. "You've been building this for years. The contract... it's just the next chapter."

She leaned into him, her body relaxing against his as if it had always been meant to be there, perfectly aligned with his. She could hear his heartbeat, a steady, rhythmic thrum beneath her cheek, and it anchored her, grounding her in the moment. The weight of the day, of the decision she had made, seemed to lift slightly as she let herself simply be—be present, be here with him, be hopeful for what lay ahead.

"I couldn't have done it without you," she whispered, the words heavy with truth. It wasn't just gratitude that filled her voice; it was a deep, unshakable knowledge that Daniel had been her rock, her steady hand guiding her through the stormy seas of uncertainty. Without him, she wasn't sure she would have had the strength to see it through.

Daniel smiled, a soft, almost imperceptible curve of his lips, and pressed a gentle kiss to the top of her head. "And I wouldn't have wanted to do anything else," he murmured, his breath warm against her hair.

In that moment, surrounded by the quiet hum of their shared space, everything seemed to align. The future, once a daunting unknown, now felt like something they could face together, one step at a time. The challenges that lay ahead no longer seemed insurmountable. They had each other. They had come this far. And now, they were ready for whatever came next.

As the weeks passed, Angela's life transformed into a whirlwind of responsibilities, a chaotic dance between meetings, looming deadlines, and decisions that seemed to come at her from every direction. The contract she had signed, the one that had once filled her with quiet excitement, now felt like a tidal wave, propelling her business into the national spotlight with an intensity she hadn't expected. What had started as a small, intimate design studio—her creative refuge—was now a hub of frenetic energy. Phones rang incessantly, fabric swatches arrived in bulk, and new hires darted between design consultations, all while Angela tried to maintain control over the growing demands of her brand. The change was palpable, and Angela could feel herself getting swept up in the storm. She had always thrived under pressure, taking pride in her ability to juggle multiple tasks and still push her creative limits. But this—this was different. Every decision felt like walking a tightrope over a chasm. One wrong step, one misplaced choice, and the entire operation could come crashing down. She felt the weight of expectations bearing down on her: the pressure from her newly hired staff who looked to her for leadership, the unspoken demands of her investors who had placed their faith—and their money—in her hands, and her own relentless drive for perfection.

Her days blurred together. Morning meetings stretched into the afternoon, punctuated only by hurried conversations about fabric shipments or last-minute adjustments to client presentations. Angela barely had time to eat, often grabbing whatever snack she could find between appointments. Her stomach had grown used to the feeling of being empty, but her mind buzzed with constant activity, refusing to slow down. And when she finally made it home at night, the familiar comfort of her apartment offered little solace. She would collapse into bed, but sleep eluded her, her thoughts racing with the hundreds of decisions still left to make. The to-do list in her mind seemed endless, always expanding, always urgent.

Daniel, too, found himself caught in the swell of his own success. What had started as a modest cleaning business, with just a few contracts and a small team, had grown exponentially, thanks in no small part to Angela's connections. Word had spread quickly in their shared circles—high-end clients, luxury hotels, and upscale office buildings were now eager to have their properties serviced by Daniel's company. The association with Angela's rising brand had brought him more business than he could have imagined, and while it was an incredible opportunity, it came with its own set of challenges.

What was once a manageable operation now required a larger workforce, spread across multiple cities. Daniel had to quickly adapt, hiring more employees, expanding his management team, and juggling contracts that came in faster than he could keep up with. His days, once simple and predictable, were now filled with back-to-back meetings, phone calls with potential clients, and constant travel between job sites to ensure that his company's standards were being upheld. He had always prided himself on being hands-on, involved in every aspect of his business, but now, with the company's rapid growth, he found himself stretched thin.

Despite their mutual success, the time Angela and Daniel once had to lean on each other grew scarce. Their cozy evenings on the couch, sharing quiet moments over a glass of wine or watching the sunset, were replaced by late nights at the office or phone calls that were cut short by yet another work emergency. They were still a team—there was no doubt about that—but the demands of their individual careers began to pull them in different directions. Conversations became rushed, brief exchanges between obligations, and they often found themselves too exhausted to talk about anything other than the latest work crisis.

One evening, as Angela sat alone in the studio, long after her employees had left for the day, she stared at the designs on her desk with a hollow feeling in her chest. The room, once buzzing with life and creativity, now felt strangely empty. The quiet wasn't comforting—it was oppressive, a reminder of how isolated she had become in the chaos of her own making. The sketches in front of her blurred as her vision fogged with exhaustion, and for the first time in weeks, she felt the creeping edge of doubt. Was this what success was supposed to feel like?

Across town, Daniel was experiencing a similar moment of reflection. Sitting in the back office of one of his new locations, he looked at the stack of contracts on his desk, each one representing another step forward, another victory. But instead of satisfaction, he felt a weariness deep in his bones. He had achieved more than he ever thought possible, but somewhere along the way, he realized he had lost something vital—the sense of purpose that had once driven him. Now, it was just about keeping up, about staying ahead of the tide. And it was exhausting.

That night, when Angela and Daniel finally made it home, they found themselves sitting in the living room, the soft glow of the lamp casting familiar shadows on the walls. But the comfort of the space, the warmth that had always been there, felt distant. Angela leaned back on the couch, her body heavy with exhaustion, while Daniel sat across from her, his own fatigue mirrored in his eyes. They exchanged a glance, both knowing that something had shifted between them, though neither had the energy to put it into words.

The champagne bottle they had once shared still sat on the shelf, unopened since that celebratory evening weeks ago. It seemed almost like a relic of a different time, a time when they had been full of hope and excitement for what the future held. Now, the future felt uncertain, and the weight of their success hung between them like a thick fog neither could see through.

Angela broke the silence first, her voice soft but tinged with the weariness she couldn't hide. "Do you ever feel like... this is all too much?"

Daniel's gaze met hers, and for a long moment, he didn't respond. But finally, he nodded, the unspoken truth settling between them. "Yeah," he admitted, his voice low. "Sometimes, I do."

In that shared vulnerability, there was a flicker of something familiar—an understanding that, despite everything pulling them in different directions, they were still in this together. But they both knew that the road ahead wouldn't be easy.

The demands of their respective businesses were slowly eroding the bond that had once been so effortless between them. Days turned into weeks, and their once comfortable rhythm had been replaced with hurried, fragmented conversations, mostly about work. The small, quiet moments of intimacy they had once cherished—the laughter shared over simple dinners, the lazy weekends spent wrapped in each other's arms—seemed like distant memories, buried beneath the weight of their careers. One night, Angela arrived home much later than she had planned. The city outside was still buzzing, but their house, usually filled with the warmth of shared time, was eerily silent. The only light was the faint glow emanating from the kitchen. She slipped off her heels, her feet aching from the long day. Her body was drained, but it wasn't just physical exhaustion—it was the kind of weariness that crept into her bones, leaving her feeling hollow. As she made her way into the kitchen, she found Daniel seated at the table, papers scattered around him, his phone glued to his ear. He looked up briefly as she entered, a small, tired smile flickering across his face before he returned to the conversation on his call. His smile was warm but weary, and something in his eyes made Angela's heart tighten.

She poured herself a glass of water and sank into the chair opposite him. The soft hum of his voice filled the space between them, but it felt distant, disconnected. Angela's gaze wandered over the papers in front of him—contracts, invoices, plans for his expanding business. She had once admired the way Daniel threw himself into his work, his passion for growing something from the ground up. But now, it seemed like both of them were trapped in a cycle of endless obligations, their personal lives overshadowed by the relentless demands of success. After what felt like an eternity, Daniel finally hung up the phone. He leaned back in his chair, pressing his fingers against his temples as if trying to massage away the stress of the day. His movements were slow, deliberate, as if even simple gestures required effort.

"Long day?" he asked, his voice edged with exhaustion.

Angela took a sip of her water, nodding. "Yeah. You?"

Daniel let out a weary laugh, though it held no real humor. "Same. It's been nonstop. I don't even know what day it is anymore." He ran a hand through his hair, his eyes drifting toward the paperwork in front of him. "Every time I think I'm caught up, something else comes up."

Angela studied him for a moment, her heart aching. He looked worn down, his face lined with the fatigue of someone who had been pushing too hard for too long. And yet, she knew she didn't look much different. The mirror had become a place she avoided—seeing the dark circles under her eyes, the way her clothes seemed to hang a little looser, a visible reminder of how much the stress was taking from her.

"We're both drowning, aren't we?" Angela said softly, her voice barely above a whisper. She hadn't meant to say it aloud, but the words slipped out before she could stop them.

Daniel looked up at her, his tired eyes meeting hers. There was a flicker of recognition in his expression, a shared understanding that they had both been avoiding. "Yeah," he admitted, his voice low. "I think we are."

Silence settled between them, heavy and unspoken. Angela glanced around the room—the same room where they had once sat, laughing over silly jokes, talking late into the night about their dreams, their future. It felt like a different life, one that had slipped through their fingers without either of them noticing.

"We can't keep going like this, Daniel," she whispered, her throat tightening with emotion. "Something has to give."

Daniel's gaze softened, and for a moment, the weight of his exhaustion seemed to lift. He reached across the table, taking her hand in his. His touch was warm, familiar, but it was laced with the same uncertainty that lingered between them. "I know," he said quietly. "But what can we do? Everything's moving so fast. It feels like... if we stop, even for a second, we'll lose everything we've worked for."

Angela squeezed his hand, her heart aching with the truth of his words. They had both worked so hard to get to this point, sacrificed so much to build their businesses, their success. But at what cost?

"I don't want to lose us," she said, her voice trembling slightly. "I don't want to wake up one day and realize we've drifted too far apart to find our way back."

Daniel's thumb brushed gently over the back of her hand. His eyes, though tired, held a glimmer of the love they had always shared. "Neither do I, Ang. We'll figure it out. We have to."

But even as he said the words, Angela couldn't shake the gnawing feeling in her chest. They had said those things before, made promises that were slowly being swallowed by the relentless tide of their ambitions. She wondered if love alone was enough to bridge the widening gap between them, or if they were simply holding on to the memory of what they used to be.

They sat there in the quiet kitchen, the hum of the city muffled through the walls, as if the world outside had paused to give them a moment of stillness. Angela's gaze drifted to the faint outlines of the streetlights casting long shadows through the curtains. For the first time in what felt like weeks, she allowed herself to truly feel the weight of everything they had been juggling—her business, his, the shared dreams that now felt more like burdens than aspirations.

"Are we doing too much?" she asked, her voice barely above a whisper, the question slipping out before she could think twice. It wasn't just about the work. It was about the way they had lost each other in the process of building lives they thought they wanted.

Daniel's eyes lifted to meet hers. There was a weariness in them that mirrored her own, but beneath the exhaustion was an understanding, a mutual recognition of the struggle they had both been trying to manage on their own. He sighed, rubbing a hand over his face before answering.

"I've been asking myself the same thing," he admitted, his voice low, edged with the fatigue that had become their constant companion. "But I think we're just doing what we have to do right now. It's a lot, but it's what we signed up for."

Angela nodded, but the truth in his words didn't ease the gnawing guilt in her chest. Yes, they had signed up for this—both of them had made choices that led them to this point. They had committed to their careers, to their dreams, but somewhere along the way, the balance had tipped. And now it felt like they were simply trying to survive the demands they had placed on themselves.

"I miss how things used to be," she said quietly, the ache in her voice palpable. "When it was just you and me, figuring things out together. Before everything got so... complicated."

Daniel's hand moved across the table, taking hers in his, the warmth of his touch a balm against the growing distance she had felt between them. His fingers wrapped around hers, a quiet but powerful reminder of the bond they still shared, even amidst the chaos.

"I miss that too," he said, his voice soft but steady. "But we'll get back to it. We just need to find our balance again."

Angela looked into his eyes, searching for the hope she had once felt so easily when they were younger, when they had nothing but each other and a belief that they could conquer anything as long as they were together. His words were reassuring, but they were also tinged with uncertainty. Neither of them knew how to find that balance again, not with the constant demands of their businesses pulling them in different directions.

But even so, there was something in Daniel's touch, in the way he looked at her, that reminded Angela of the foundation they had built together. The life they had once dreamed of wasn't completely lost. It had just been buried under layers of ambition, under the pressure to succeed, to prove something to themselves and to the world.

"We'll figure it out," Daniel said, his thumb gently stroking the back of her hand. "It's just going to take some time."

Angela nodded again, but this time there was a flicker of hope beneath the guilt. Maybe it wouldn't be easy. Maybe it would take time and effort, more than either of them had anticipated. But if they could still sit here, across from each other in this quiet kitchen, with all the weight of their lives pressing down on them, and still reach for each other—then maybe they hadn't lost everything after all.

"Yeah," she whispered, her voice a little stronger. "We will."

Angela's life, once driven by passion and purpose, had begun to feel like an endless marathon, one in which she couldn't seem to find her stride. The weeks following the signing of the contract passed in a haze of meetings, fabric samples, press releases, and constant demands for her attention. Her calendar was packed; every minute accounted for by someone else's need for her time or approval. She moved through her days mechanically, as if on autopilot, constantly pulled between design approvals and conference calls, the days bleeding into nights until she barely remembered what a full night's rest felt like.

On paper, everything looked perfect—her business was thriving, gaining national recognition, and she was being hailed as a rising star in the fashion world. But inside, a gnawing unease had started to fester.

It began as a faint, almost unnoticeable discomfort in her chest one evening while she sat at her desk, surrounded by invoices and supplier agreements. She dismissed it at first—chalked it up to stress, a familiar companion over the last several months. Angela stretched, rolling her shoulders back to relieve the tension, but the tightness persisted, a dull ache that seemed to deepen with every breath. She sipped at her water, willing herself to push through it, but the feeling lingered, like a heavy weight pressing down on her ribcage.

She pressed her palm flat against her chest, trying to soothe the ache beneath the skin, but instead, her heart raced beneath her fingers, pounding in a way that felt urgent, wrong. Her breaths came shallow, each one feeling shorter than the last. Anxiety flickered at the edge of her mind, but she shoved it aside. *Not now, I don't have time for this*, she thought, forcing herself to focus back on the task at hand.

That night, she came home long after the city had gone quiet, the house still and dark except for the soft glow of a lamp in the hallway. Daniel was already asleep, his breathing steady and slow, a soft reminder of the life they had built together. She slipped into bed beside him, careful not to disturb his sleep, but as she lay there, the ache in her chest intensified, expanding outward until it felt like a band tightening around her lungs. She tried to calm herself, counting her breaths, telling herself it was just exhaustion, but her heart raced on, beating a frantic rhythm that kept her wide awake.

Angela considered waking Daniel, but stopped herself. He was already juggling so much with his own business, which had exploded in growth almost overnight. She didn't want to add to his stress. Instead, she lay in the dark, staring at the ceiling, her mind swirling with thoughts of everything that needed to be done tomorrow, the list growing longer with each passing minute.

Sleep eluded her, and when she finally drifted off, it was fitful, her mind running in circles even in her dreams.

As the days passed, the tightness in her chest didn't go away. It grew worse. At first, she managed to ignore it, pushing through the discomfort, but soon it became impossible to pretend everything was fine. Some days, she found herself gasping for air, the room spinning as if the walls were closing in around her. Her once-sharp focus had dulled, replaced by the pounding headaches that often blurred her vision. She had to step away from her work for hours at a time, retreating to the quiet of her office or even the bathroom just to escape the noise and pressure of her growing responsibilities. Still, she didn't say anything. Not to Daniel, not to her team. Everyone around her was relying on her, and Angela had never been one to let people down. She'd fought too hard for this. She had sacrificed too much. But as each day passed, the signs became harder to ignore. The chest pains, the shortness of breath, the debilitating headaches. They were all there, warning her that something wasn't right, that she was pushing herself too far. But Angela kept going, telling herself that she didn't have time to stop—not now, not when everything she had worked for was finally within reach.

Angela's world felt slow and distant as she blinked through the haze of her hospital room. Her body was heavy, each breath an effort, but the stabbing pain in her chest had dulled to a lingering ache. She shifted slightly, feeling the tug of the IV in her arm, and the sterile coldness of the hospital bed beneath her. Daniel sat beside her, his face etched with worry, his hands clasped together as if he was holding himself together by sheer will. His eyes were tired, the dark circles beneath them betraying the sleepless hours he must have spent waiting. Angela tried to smile, but it felt weak and strained, as though even that small gesture required more energy than she had.

"Hey," she whispered, her voice rasping as she spoke. "How long have I been here?"

"A few hours," Daniel replied softly, leaning closer. His hand reached out, covering hers, his warmth reassuring, grounding her. "They ran some tests, said it was exhaustion and stress-induced. But... they also want to keep you here overnight for more observations. You collapsed, Ang. You weren't breathing right."

She could hear the tremble in his voice, the fear he was trying to mask with calmness. Angela swallowed, her throat dry, the gravity of what had happened finally sinking in. She had pushed herself too far. Ignoring the warning signs, denying the pain—it had all caught up with her.

"I'm sorry," she whispered, her eyes filling with tears she hadn't expected. She hated seeing Daniel like this, filled with so much concern. "I didn't want to worry you."

Daniel's brow furrowed, and he shook his head, gripping her hand a little tighter. "Worry me? Angela, you *collapsed*. I've been watching you burn yourself out for weeks. I knew you were struggling, but... I didn't think it would get this bad. Why didn't you tell me?"

She stared at him, the guilt coiling in her chest, heavier than the exhaustion she felt. "I thought I could handle it. Everything was going so well, and I just didn't want to slow down. I didn't want to let anyone down, especially you."

Daniel exhaled sharply, his voice steady but filled with emotion. "You're not letting me down. You've never let me down. But this—pushing yourself to the point where you collapse—it's not worth it. None of it is worth losing you."

His words hit her harder than the pain ever had. Angela closed her eyes, tears slipping down her cheeks as the truth settled in. She had been so focused on achieving success, on living up to the expectations of her business, her staff, her investors, that she had forgotten the most important thing—herself. And the people she loved.

"I can't keep going like this, can I?" she whispered, the realization heavy in her chest.

Daniel gently wiped away her tears, his voice soft but firm. "No, you can't. We can't. We're both stretched too thin. I've been too busy too, and we've let this... this craziness take over everything." He paused, his voice catching. "We need to find a way out of this before we lose each other. Before you lose yourself."

Angela's heart ached, but not from the exhaustion this time. It was the pain of recognizing how far they had drifted, how their once-strong bond had been tested by their relentless ambition. She nodded, feeling the weight of his words sink in.

"I don't want to lose you," she said, her voice barely above a whisper.

"You won't," Daniel promised, his fingers brushing lightly against her cheek. "We'll figure this out. Together. We just need to slow down, make time for us. For you."

The enormity of everything she had been carrying—her business, her dreams, the expectations she had set for herself—began to lift, just a little. Angela looked at Daniel, her partner, her anchor, and realized that maybe, just maybe, she didn't have to do it all alone.

"I'll try," she murmured, the exhaustion seeping back into her bones, though this time it felt less overwhelming. "I'll try to slow down."

Daniel pressed a gentle kiss to her forehead. "That's all I need from you. We'll figure the rest out."

Angela's voice wavered as she spoke, the frustration bubbling beneath the surface. She set her cup down on the table with a dull thud, her fingers trembling slightly. Daniel watched her, the concern in his eyes deepening. He understood how much she had sacrificed to get to where she was—how relentless she had been, always pushing herself beyond her limits. It was one of the things he admired most about her, but now it felt like that very drive was eating her alive.

"I get it," Daniel said, his voice low but steady. He reached across the table, his hand covering hers. "But if you don't take a step back, you're going to burn out completely. What happens to everything you've built then?"

Angela's breath hitched, and for the first time in days, she let herself feel the full weight of it all—the crushing pressure of expectations, the fear of failure looming just over the horizon. She blinked rapidly, willing away the tears that threatened to fall. She wasn't someone who cried easily, but lately, everything felt too much, like the world was pressing down on her chest.

"I don't want to lose this," she whispered, her gaze fixed on the dark surface of her coffee. "I've worked too hard to lose it all now."

"You won't," Daniel reassured her, squeezing her hand gently. "But you've got to trust that things will still move forward, even if you take a step back. You've built something strong enough to withstand a little pause. It's not all on you anymore."

Angela let out a bitter laugh, shaking her head. "It sure feels like it's all on me. There's always something—some problem, some decision that only I can make. Everyone's counting on me."

Daniel leaned forward, his voice firmer now. "But what about *you*, Ang? When was the last time you counted on anyone else?"

Angela blinked, taken aback by his words. She opened her mouth to respond, but nothing came out. He was right. For so long, she had been the one people leaned on—her staff, her clients, even Daniel at times. She had taken it upon herself to carry everyone's weight, never asking for help, never allowing herself the luxury of rest. She looked at Daniel, his tired eyes mirroring her own exhaustion, and something shifted inside her. She realized she wasn't the only one struggling. He had been there beside her the whole time, dealing with his own battles, but always making sure she had someone to lean on. And she had taken that for granted, assuming she had to do it all alone.

"I don't know how to let go," she finally admitted, her voice cracking. "I've always been the one in control."

"You don't have to do it all on your own," Daniel said gently. "You've got a whole team now. You've built something incredible. It's okay to lean on them. And on me."

She looked up at him, the man who had been by her side through everything—the man who had always believed in her, even when she didn't believe in herself. "What would I do without you?"

"You won't ever have to find out," he said with a soft smile. "We're in this together, remember?"

CHAPTER 8

Just as Angela had begun to focus on her recovery, Daniel's world shifted yet again. It was late in the evening, the house enveloped in an unsettling quiet. Angela was resting in the other room, her breathing soft and steady as she slept, trying to heal. Daniel, sitting alone at the dining table, was attempting to catch up on a mountain of emails, mindlessly sifting through them, when his phone buzzed beside him. The vibration cut through the stillness, jarring him out of the mundane tasks he had been occupying himself with. He glanced at the screen, noting an unfamiliar number. His instinct told him to ignore it, but something in the back of his mind wouldn't let it go. There was a nagging sensation, a whisper of recognition he couldn't quite place.

With a sigh, Daniel picked up the phone, his voice cautious but firm. "Hello?"

The voice on the other end was smooth, too familiar for comfort, and carried with it the weight of old ghosts. "Daniel? It's been a long time."

That chill of recognition settled deep in Daniel's spine, cold and sharp. He knew who it was before the man even said his name. *Eric Price.* The man who had once been his business partner, the same man who had come dangerously close to ruining Daniel's life when they ran a cleaning company together. Eric's shady deals, reckless decisions, and utter disregard for anything but his own gain had nearly sunk the company—and Daniel along with it.

Daniel's grip tightened around his phone, his voice hardening with the memory. "What do you want, Eric?"

A low chuckle came through the line, the kind that reminded Daniel just how manipulative Eric had always been. He wasn't someone who played by the rules, not unless he was the one making them. "Is that any way to greet an old friend? I heard about your little empire. Looks like you've done pretty well for yourself. Cleaning houses for the rich and famous, huh?"

The mention of Daniel's business, the life he had rebuilt brick by brick after their fallout, set his teeth on edge. He had worked too hard to get where he was, and Eric had no right to even speak of it.

"What do you want?" Daniel repeated, his tone clipped, each word dripping with disdain. There was a pause on the other end, a dangerous silence that stretched just a little too long, the kind that made Daniel's skin crawl. Eric's voice, when it finally returned, was laced with something darker, more calculated. "I think you owe me, Daniel. You wouldn't be where you are now without me."

Daniel's jaw clenched. Typical Eric, twisting reality to suit his narrative. The man had always been a master at turning the tables, making you second-guess your own memory, your own truth. But Daniel remembered everything. He remembered the sleepless nights, the financial wreckage, and the betrayal. He remembered how close he had come to losing everything. "I don't owe you anything. You screwed me over, and we both know it."

Eric's reply was as slick as oil. "That's not how I remember it. But I'll cut to the chase." He paused again, as if savoring the moment. "I want in on your business. A partnership. We could do great things together, just like the old days."

The sheer audacity of the proposal made Daniel's heart pound in his chest. His pulse quickened, the anger simmering just beneath the surface threatening to boil over. He could feel his muscles tense, his free hand curling into a fist at his side. "You've got to be kidding me," Daniel said, voice low and dangerous. "I'm not letting you anywhere near my business."

The shift in Eric's tone was immediate. The smooth charm evaporated, replaced by something far more sinister. "I wouldn't be so quick to dismiss me," he said, his voice hard now, the edges sharp enough to cut. "I know things, Daniel. Things that could cause a lot of problems for you. You might want to reconsider."

Daniel shot up from his chair, pacing the room with restless energy, his mind racing. He had known this was coming, some part of him had always known. Eric wasn't the type to disappear quietly into the background. He was like a shadow, lurking, waiting for the right moment to re-emerge. And now, with everything finally coming together in Daniel's life—his business thriving, Angela recovering—Eric had decided to rear his head. It was like a snake slithering back into his life, ready to strike.

He glanced toward the closed bedroom door where Angela was resting. Just the thought of Eric bringing his chaos into their lives made Daniel's stomach twist. He had worked too hard, fought too long, to let someone like Eric threaten it all. The anger burning in his chest wasn't just about his business or the betrayal from years ago. It was about protecting what mattered now. Angela. Their future. Everything he had rebuilt.

But Eric had always been good at finding weaknesses, and the way he spoke, with that dangerous undertone, made it clear he was ready to exploit any he could find.

"You stay away from me and my family, Eric," Daniel growled, his voice hard and filled with a quiet, simmering rage. He could feel his pulse thrumming in his temples, his grip tightening around the phone as if it might somehow translate his anger through the device. "Or you'll regret it."

On the other end of the line, Eric let out a low, dark chuckle, the kind that made Daniel's skin crawl. "We'll see about that," Eric said, his words dripping with ominous promise.

And then, with a soft click, the call was over.

Daniel stood frozen in place, the phone still pressed against his ear as if he hadn't yet registered that the conversation had ended. Eric's voice, slick and threatening, echoed in his head, stirring up memories he had spent years trying to bury. The familiar dread washed over him, the kind that had haunted him when his first business had nearly collapsed under the weight of Eric's recklessness. He had clawed his way back from the edge, rebuilding his life, brick by painstaking brick, but now it felt as though the past was slithering back into his life, ready to tear everything apart once again. Slowly, he lowered the phone, placing it on the table with a deliberate calm that belied the turmoil inside him. His hand moved to his hair, raking through it as if the action might somehow untangle the mess of emotions—anger, fear, frustration—that were currently warring within him. The thought of telling Angela about Eric filled him with a sense of dread that had nothing to do with his own pride or the potential threat to his business. She was still recovering, fragile in ways she rarely let show. The last thing she needed was the weight of this looming over her, the stress of knowing that someone like Eric Price was sniffing around their lives again. But as much as he wanted to shield her from it, keeping this from her felt just as wrong. She deserved to know. She always had, and part of what had made their relationship work was that they never kept secrets from each other. Even now, as he stood at the edge of a potential storm, Daniel knew he couldn't go back on that.

Taking a deep breath, he set the phone aside and turned toward the window, letting his gaze drift over the city lights in the distance. The view always brought him a strange sense of calm, the way the lights twinkled like stars against the darkness, but tonight, even that couldn't settle the knot forming in his gut. Eric was a wildcard, the kind of person who thrived in chaos, feeding off of other people's weaknesses. Daniel had learned the hard way never to underestimate him. He knew better than to dismiss Eric's threats as empty. If Eric said he could cause problems, it meant he was already thinking of ways to do it. Daniel couldn't afford to be caught off guard. He had worked too damn hard to let someone like Eric ruin everything—not again. Not when he had fought tooth and nail to get where he was now. But this time, Daniel wasn't the same man he'd been years ago. He was smarter, more cautious, and he had resources now. He had built something real, something solid. And he wasn't about to let it all come crashing down.

He needed a plan. First thing in the morning, he would call his legal team. Make sure every corner of his business was secure, every loophole closed. If Eric tried to stir up trouble, Daniel would be ready. He'd have the legal firepower to push back, to protect what he had built. But even as he mapped out his next moves, the thought of Eric's reappearance lingered like a dark cloud on the horizon. And then there was Angela. He couldn't— wouldn't—keep this from her. But how was he supposed to bring it up without worrying her, without adding to her burden while she was still in recovery? His stomach twisted at the thought of seeing the concern in her eyes, the stress tightening her already frail body. He sighed, the weight of the situation pressing down on him like a physical force. Quietly, Daniel made his way toward the bedroom, his footsteps soft against the hardwood floor. As he reached the door, he paused, leaning against the frame as he watched Angela sleep. The room was dim, the soft glow of the moon casting a gentle light across her face. She was curled up beneath the blankets, her breathing steady and peaceful, her chest rising and falling with a soothing rhythm. For a moment, the storm brewing in Daniel's mind faded, and all he could think about was how much he loved her.

This was why he fought. This was what mattered most. Not the business, not the money, but Angela, and the life they had built together. The future they had planned. And no one—not Eric, not anyone—was going to take that away from him.

With a quiet determination, Daniel slipped into bed beside her. He lay there for a moment, his eyes tracing the outline of her form beneath the blankets, the sound of her breathing grounding him in a way nothing else could. His mind, though still racing, began to settle, his thoughts organizing themselves into a singular focus. As he closed his eyes, Daniel made a silent vow: no matter what Eric was planning, no matter what threats he made, Daniel would do whatever it took to protect what mattered most. He had been through hell before, and he had come out the other side stronger. He wasn't about to let anyone—especially someone like Eric Price—destroy the life he had fought so hard to rebuild.

Eric might think he could shake things up, that he could manipulate the situation to his advantage, but this time, Daniel was ready. Whatever came next, he would face it head-on. He had no choice.

Days passed, but the unease that Eric's call had stirred in Daniel lingered like a persistent shadow, creeping into the corners of his mind no matter how hard he tried to shake it. Each morning, he woke before dawn, the oppressive weight of Eric's words pressing down on his chest, suffocating the brief moments of peace sleep might have given him. He made every effort to maintain a façade of normalcy, not wanting to add to the burden Angela was already carrying. She had enough on her plate, still recovering, still fragile in ways that were hard to admit. But Daniel's attempts to keep things under control were starting to crack. The changes were subtle at first. He was quieter around the house, his usual easygoing demeanor dulled by the stress gnawing at him. He spent more time in his own head, retreating into his thoughts whenever the weight of the situation became too heavy to bear. More often than not, Angela would catch him staring off into space, his brow furrowed in deep thought, his mind replaying Eric's threats over and over again, searching for some kind of solution, some way to protect what he had worked so hard to build. One evening, after another long day spent managing his expanding cleaning contracts, Daniel found himself lying awake, staring at the ceiling in the dark. Angela was asleep beside him, her breathing slow and steady, a soft rhythm that should have been comforting. But for Daniel, the silence felt suffocating, the air thick with the weight of everything he hadn't told her. The house seemed too quiet, the stillness only amplifying the thoughts racing through his mind. He couldn't shake the feeling that the walls were closing in, that Eric's presence, even from a distance, was somehow tightening its grip around his life.

He wanted to believe that Eric's call had been nothing more than a desperate attempt at stirring up old trouble, that it was all empty threats meant to rattle him. But deep down, Daniel knew better. Eric wasn't the type to make idle threats. He was the kind of man who thrived on control, on using other people's fears and weaknesses to his advantage. And that's what kept Daniel up at night—the possibility that Eric wasn't bluffing. That the man really did know something, some hidden detail from their shared past that could be used to wreak havoc on Daniel's life.

Careful not to wake Angela, Daniel shifted out of bed and padded downstairs. The kitchen, normally a place of calm and routine, felt like a temporary refuge from the storm brewing in his mind. He poured himself a glass of water, his hand trembling slightly as he lifted it to his lips. The cool liquid did little to settle his nerves. This was no way to live—trapped between protecting Angela from the truth and the crushing realization that he couldn't do it alone.

He had to tell her. There was no other way.

Just as Daniel set the glass down, Angela appeared in the doorway, her silhouette softly illuminated by the faint glow of the moonlight filtering in through the window. She rubbed her eyes, her hair tousled from sleep, but the concern on her face was unmistakable.

"Couldn't sleep?" she asked, her voice still thick with drowsiness but laced with the quiet worry she had been carrying for days.

Daniel let out a long, heavy sigh, running a hand through his hair in a gesture that had become all too familiar. "No," he admitted, his voice barely above a whisper. "Too much on my mind."

Angela crossed the room, her bare feet making no sound on the cool tile floor, and came to stand beside him. Her hand rested gently on his arm, offering comfort in the way only she could. "You've been distracted lately," she said softly, her eyes searching his face for answers. "Is everything okay?"

The question hit him like a punch to the gut. He hesitated, the words stuck in his throat as he struggled with how to begin. How could he explain everything without overwhelming her, without adding more weight to the load she was already carrying? But he knew he couldn't keep this from her any longer. Not when it had the potential to upend both of their lives.

"There's something I need to tell you," Daniel said at last, his voice low, as though speaking the words too loudly might make the situation more real, more dangerous. He turned to face her, the kitchen suddenly feeling smaller, more confined. "I got a call the other day... from someone I used to know. My old business partner."

Angela's brow furrowed in confusion, her gaze sharpening as concern flickered across her features. "Business partner? I didn't know you had a partner."

Daniel sighed again, leaning against the counter, running his hand through his hair once more as he prepared himself for the full story. "It was a long time ago," he said, his tone distant, as if recalling a bad dream. "Before I met you. We started the cleaning business together, but it didn't last. He was reckless, made bad deals, cut corners—nearly ran the whole thing into the ground. I had to break ties with him, and it wasn't exactly a clean split." He paused, the memories flooding back, each one heavier than the last. "We haven't spoken in years."

Angela's concern deepened as she listened, her hand still resting on his arm, her eyes searching his face for the full truth. "And now he's calling you? After all this time?"

Daniel nodded, feeling the weight of the situation settle more heavily between them. "Yeah. He's... not the type to just call out of the blue. He wants something, and I'm pretty sure it's not just to catch up."

Angela crossed her arms, her expression hardening as she processed what Daniel was saying. There was a cautiousness in her eyes, the same kind she had whenever she sensed danger lurking beneath the surface. "What does he want now?"

Daniel's stomach knotted as Eric's veiled threat played over in his mind, like a persistent echo he couldn't shake. "He says I owe him. That without him, I wouldn't have made it this far— that he deserves a cut of what I've built. And if I don't give him what he wants, he's going to cause trouble. He didn't go into detail, but knowing Eric, it's going to be bad."

Angela's eyes narrowed, her voice steady but with a sharp edge. "You can't give in to him, Daniel. He has no claim to your business or anything you've worked for."

"I know," Daniel said, frustration creeping into his voice, his fists clenching at the thought of Eric's audacity. "But I also know how he operates. He's manipulative, and he's not afraid to use whatever leverage he has to get what he wants. It doesn't matter if it's legal or not—he'll find some way to make my life hell. And if he goes public with whatever dirt he thinks he has, it could hurt us. Not just the business, but everything we've worked for. Our reputation, the clients, maybe even personal stuff…"

Angela let out a breath, her anger giving way to concern as she reached for his hand, wrapping her fingers around his in a gentle but firm grip. "We'll handle this together," she said, her tone soft but determined. "We've faced worse, and we'll figure out a way to make sure he can't touch us. But don't keep this from me, okay? We're a team, Daniel. We fight these battles together."

Daniel felt a surge of emotion swell in his chest, a mix of gratitude and relief. He had been carrying the weight of Eric's threat on his own for days, letting it fester inside him, but now, just having Angela's support made it feel a little more manageable, like the pressure had been lifted, if only slightly.

He gave her hand a squeeze, nodding. "I won't. I should've told you sooner."

Angela's gaze lingered on him, her eyes filled with understanding, but beneath it all, there was an unspoken readiness for whatever was coming. She wasn't one to shy away from a fight, and Daniel knew that with her by his side, he stood a better chance against whatever Eric had in store.

But as they stood together in the quiet kitchen, the low hum of the refrigerator the only sound breaking the stillness, Daniel couldn't shake the feeling that this was only the beginning. Eric was the kind of man who didn't make idle threats. He played the long game, and the storm he had warned about was likely already on the horizon, gathering strength. It wasn't just the business at risk—Daniel could sense that this time, Eric's reach could extend further, into the very fabric of their lives, threatening to tear down everything they had built together.

Daniel looked at Angela, her eyes unwavering as she stood beside him, and he knew they had to be careful. If they weren't, Eric Price would find a way to unravel it all.

The next morning, Daniel woke with a renewed sense of determination coursing through his veins. The early light filtering through the blinds cast long shadows across the room, but Daniel's thoughts were already sharp, focused. He wasn't going to let Eric derail the life he had fought so hard to build. Not after everything he and Angela had sacrificed, after all the battles they had already won. As soon as he had dressed, he began reaching out to his network of legal contacts. He knew he had to move quickly, quietly, and strategically. Eric wasn't one to make idle threats, and Daniel had no illusions about the man's willingness to twist the law to his advantage. This wouldn't be a simple dispute; it was going to be war. Daniel wasn't about to be caught unprepared. His legal team needed to be airtight, ready to counter every baseless claim Eric might throw their way. Still, Daniel chose not to burden Angela with every detail. He kept her in the loop where it mattered, letting her know the broad strokes of what was happening, but he didn't want to overwhelm her. She had enough on her plate. Some battles, Daniel reasoned, were his to fight alone. Meanwhile, Angela was working through her own struggle. Her recovery was slow, but steady, as she followed her doctor's advice to reduce stress and rest. It wasn't easy for her— Angela had never been one to sit back and let others take the reins. She had built her design business from the ground up, just like Daniel had built his, and stepping back wasn't in her nature. But her health was at stake, and she knew that delegating more to her growing team of designers and managers wasn't just necessary—it was critical for the future of her business and their life together.

Still, a restlessness gnawed at her. Angela could sense the tension in the air, an unspoken feeling that something darker was looming, just out of sight. And she wasn't wrong.

It was a Wednesday afternoon when the letter arrived. The envelope was crisp, the address neatly printed in a formal script. Daniel opened it at the kitchen counter, expecting nothing more than a routine piece of mail—perhaps a bill or some trivial business correspondence.

But as his eyes scanned the document, his face drained of color. His hand tightened around the paper, gripping it harder than he realized.

"Daniel?" Angela's voice was sharp with concern. She watched him closely, her eyes narrowing as his expression shifted. "What is it?"

Without a word, Daniel handed her the letter, the shock still sinking in like a slow, cold wave.

Angela's eyes darted across the page. At first, she didn't understand what she was seeing—legal jargon that blurred into meaninglessness. But then it hit her. Her breath caught in her throat as the words crystallized: *A demand for arbitration.* Eric Price was claiming that he was entitled to a portion of Daniel's business profits, citing a partnership agreement that had long since been buried in the rubble of their severed ties.

"This is insane," Angela said, her voice shaking with disbelief. She tossed the letter onto the counter, the paper landing with a light thud, but the weight of the situation was much heavier. "He can't do this."

"He thinks he can," Daniel muttered, his voice tight with anger as he ran a hand over his jaw, clenching his teeth. His eyes flicked back to the letter, the disgust evident in his furrowed brow. "And if this drags into court, it could get ugly. He doesn't care about the business or the money. He just wants to hurt me—to take something from me, like he's done before."

Angela's fingers curled into fists as she stared at the letter, her pulse quickening. The anger was sharp, hot in her chest, but underneath it, a gnawing fear took root. This was more than just a legal dispute—it was a personal attack, and one that had the potential to rip apart everything they had worked for. She could see it in Daniel's face too—the determination, yes, but also the weariness. He knew what was coming, and so did she.

"We need a lawyer," Angela said, her voice firm. "A damn good one."

"I've already got someone working on it," Daniel replied, though the tension in his tone betrayed his frustration. He let out a slow breath, glancing out the window as if searching for clarity. "But this... it's going to be a fight, Ang. It's not going to be quick. And it's not going to be clean."

Angela crossed the room and stood beside him, her hand slipping into his. "Then we fight," she said simply, her voice steady despite the storm brewing inside her. She gave his hand a squeeze, and Daniel turned to look at her, the hint of a grim smile tugging at the corner of his mouth.

They were in this together, and no matter how long or difficult the fight would be, they wouldn't let Eric Price tear apart the life they had built. The stakes were too high, and they both knew it. But as they stood side by side in the quiet of their kitchen, a silent understanding passed between them.

This wasn't just about business anymore. This was personal.

Angela nodded, her mind racing with the implications. They had fought so hard to get to where they were, and now it felt like it could all slip through their fingers because of one man's greed. But as much as the fear gnawed at her, a steely resolve began to take root. They had faced bigger challenges before—personal, financial, and emotional. They could get through this too. As the days wore on, Daniel and Angela found themselves increasingly preoccupied with Eric's looming threat. The legal process was slow and grueling, each new letter or phone call from their attorney dragging the matter out longer than either of them could bear. Every moment of calm was tinged with the uncertainty of what would happen next, but life continued moving forward regardless. Daniel had begun to hire more staff for his cleaning business, stepping back from the day-to-day operations so that he could focus on the legal battle with Eric. Angela, in turn, continued to recover her strength and returned to designing, slowly finding her rhythm again. They leaned on each other more than ever, their bond growing stronger with each passing day. But there was an unspoken tension between them, the kind that comes from being on the edge of a precipice. Neither of them wanted to admit how scared they were of what the future might hold. One evening, after a particularly exhausting meeting with their attorney, Daniel and Angela sat on the couch, their usual quiet replaced by a heavy, unspoken tension.

"I keep thinking about what would happen if Eric actually won," Daniel confessed, breaking the silence.

Angela looked at him, her eyes searching his face. "He's not going to win, Daniel. We won't let him."

"I know," Daniel sighed. "But the thought is still there, you know? What if we lose everything we've worked for? What if he drags us through the mud, takes everything from us? I can't shake it."

Angela leaned in, her voice firm. "Listen to me. We've built this together. We've overcome every challenge, every obstacle. Eric can throw whatever he wants at us, but he's not stronger than us. And he doesn't have what we have. We've built something real, something solid. He can't take that away."

Daniel gazed into her eyes, the depth of her belief in them pulling him from the dark spiral he'd been caught in. He nodded slowly, squeezing her hand. "You're right. I just… I don't want to lose what we've got. I don't want to lose you."

"You won't," she whispered, her voice steady. "We're in this together. No matter what."

The legal battle with Eric escalated in the following weeks. Every day brought a new challenge—another letter, another request for documentation, another veiled threat from his lawyer. Daniel found himself living in two worlds: one where he tried to manage his business and protect his newfound life with Angela, and another where he was constantly looking over his shoulder, waiting for Eric's next move. It was a Friday evening when Daniel received a call from his attorney. The sun had just set, casting long shadows across their backyard as Daniel paced, phone in hand. Angela was in the kitchen, preparing dinner, her mind occupied with the new designs she was working on. She watched him through the window, noticing the tension in his posture.

"Are you sure?" Daniel's voice was strained, disbelief lacing his words.

The attorney's response was muffled, but whatever was said left Daniel standing still, staring into the fading light. He ended the call, his hands trembling slightly as he placed the phone on the counter. Angela walked outside, drying her hands on a dish towel, her concern deepening.

"What happened?" she asked softly, already sensing that it wasn't good news.

Daniel turned to her, his face pale. "He's not just going after the business anymore. He's claiming that I defrauded him—says I stole money when I left the partnership. He's trying to paint me as a criminal."

Angela's heart sank. "That's ridiculous. There's no way he can prove something that isn't true."

"I know," Daniel said, frustration boiling over. "But he's not trying to prove anything. He just wants to drag me through the mud, ruin my reputation. If this gets out, it'll be all over the media. I could lose clients, contracts... everything."

Angela's jaw tightened as she felt the rising anger in her chest. Eric wasn't just trying to take what didn't belong to him—he was trying to destroy Daniel, his business, and everything they'd built together. It wasn't just about money anymore. It was personal.

"We'll fight this," Angela said firmly, stepping closer. "We're not going to let him win. He can throw whatever he wants at us, but we're not backing down."

Daniel looked at her, his eyes heavy with fear and exhaustion. "I don't know if we can fight this, Ang. He's got money, connections... and if this gets to court, it could drag on for years."

Angela's voice softened, but her resolve didn't waver. "We've been through worse. This is just another challenge. We're going to get through it."

Daniel nodded slowly, wanting to believe her. But the weight of Eric's attack was growing heavier, and he couldn't shake the feeling that no matter what they did, there would be scars left behind. As the legal storm raged on, Daniel found himself thinking more and more about his past with Eric. He hadn't spoken much about that time in his life to Angela or anyone else for that matter. It was a chapter he'd buried, locked away in the recesses of his mind, believing it was better left forgotten. But now, as Eric forced his way back into his life, those memories were coming to the surface whether Daniel liked it or not. There was a time when Daniel and Eric had been close—partners in more than just business. They'd grown up together, attended the same high school, and while their paths had diverged after graduation, they reunited years later with a shared dream of building a cleaning empire. Back then, Eric had been charming, ambitious, and persuasive. He could talk anyone into anything, and Daniel admired his confidence. But as time passed, Eric's charm revealed a darker side. He cut corners, made deals that put their business at risk, and engaged in activities that Daniel wanted no part of. When Daniel discovered that Eric had been skimming profits and using their company as a front for shady dealings, it was the final straw. Daniel had walked away from the partnership, leaving everything behind, but Eric had never forgiven him for it.

Now, all those years later, Eric was back for revenge.

One evening, after an exhausting day of meetings with lawyers and accountants, Daniel sat on the porch with Angela. The air was warm, and the faint hum of cicadas filled the silence between them.

"I've been thinking a lot about Eric," Daniel admitted, staring out into the darkening sky. "About how we used to be friends. How everything got so messed up."

Angela shifted in her chair, listening intently. She could hear the pain in his voice, the conflict between regret and anger.

"We started the business together," Daniel continued, his voice low. "At first, it was great. We had big dreams, and for a while, it felt like we were on top of the world. But then Eric… he changed. Or maybe he didn't change—maybe I just didn't see him for who he really was until it was too late."

Angela reached for his hand, squeezing it gently. "What happened between you two?"

Daniel sighed, his mind drifting back to those days. "He started making deals behind my back, shady contracts with people who were involved in things I didn't want to know about. When I found out, I told him I couldn't be part of it. I walked away. I thought that would be the end of it, but Eric… he's always been the kind of guy who holds a grudge. I just didn't think he'd come back after all these years."

Angela's brow furrowed. "Do you think he's still involved in that kind of business?"

Daniel shrugged. "I don't know. But I wouldn't be surprised. He's always been about power and money, and he'll do whatever it takes to get it."

Angela was quiet for a moment, processing everything Daniel had shared. "You did the right thing by walking away. You couldn't have known he'd come after you like this."

"I know," Daniel said, though the guilt still gnawed at him. "But now it feels like everything's falling apart because of a decision I made years ago."

Angela turned to face him, her eyes filled with determination. "This isn't your fault. Eric's the one who's trying to destroy us, not you. And we're going to fight back. You've built something amazing, and no one—not even Eric—can take that away."

Daniel nodded, though the fear still lingered at the edges of his mind. He just hoped that Angela's faith in him, in them, would be enough to see them through the storm.

Days turned into weeks, and the legal battle with Eric consumed nearly every aspect of their lives. The strain was starting to show—Daniel was more exhausted than ever, spending long nights going through old records and paperwork, preparing for every possible move Eric might make. Angela, too, felt the weight of it all, though she did her best to stay strong for both of them. One afternoon, as they sat with their attorney, reviewing the latest documents Eric's legal team had sent over, Daniel's phone buzzed. He glanced down at the screen and froze.

It was a message from his ex-wife, Beth.

I need to talk. It's important.

Daniel's stomach dropped. He hadn't heard from Beth in years, not since the divorce. She'd made it clear that she wanted nothing to do with him, moving on with her new life and leaving him to pick up the pieces.

Angela noticed the change in his expression and leaned over to see the message. Her face tightened, but she didn't say anything. She didn't have to.

"What does she want?" Angela asked, her tone neutral but wary.

"I don't know," Daniel said, frowning at the screen. "But I'm sure it's nothing good."

Angela didn't respond right away, but Daniel could see the tension building in her posture. She trusted him, but the idea of Beth reaching out—especially now, with everything else going on—was unsettling.

Daniel typed a quick reply, asking Beth what she wanted. Minutes later, the response came:

I think it's time we talked about the kids.

Daniel's heart raced. The kids—his children from his first marriage, who he hadn't seen in years. The divorce had been messy, and Beth had taken them with her when she left, making it nearly impossible for Daniel to stay in their lives.

Angela looked at him, her expression unreadable. "What are you going to do?"

"I don't know," Daniel admitted. "But I can't ignore this."

CHAPTER 9

Daniel stared at the phone, his mind spinning. It had been years since he'd had any real contact with Beth. After the divorce, she had made sure to keep their children out of his reach. For a long time, it was easier that way—less painful to stay away than to be in and out of their lives. But now, here she was, reappearing just when everything was falling apart. Angela watched him carefully, her eyes full of questions. She could sense the weight of the decision Daniel was about to make, and it wasn't an easy one. The mention of his kids was like a punch to the gut—Daniel had never stopped thinking about them, even if he'd stopped fighting to see them.

"What does she really want, Daniel?" Angela's voice was calm but firm, the underlying concern evident.

"I don't know," Daniel said quietly, feeling the weight of regret and uncertainty crushing him. "But I have to find out."

Angela nodded, although her eyes lingered on him with worry. She knew this was bigger than just Beth reaching out. It wasn't just a conversation—it was a reminder of everything Daniel had lost, a door opening to a past he hadn't fully dealt with. And now, in the midst of Eric's attack and their fragile business, Beth's timing felt like another challenge on top of everything else. Daniel sat down, running his hands through his hair, the memories of his old life flooding back. He remembered the early days of his marriage to Beth. They were both young, filled with the kind of optimism that comes with building a life together. But as the years passed, the cracks slowly started to show. He was consumed by work, trying to build a career to support their family, while Beth seemed to want something else—something more. She was always chasing after the next thrill, the next adventure, and eventually, that led her straight into the arms of a younger man. The divorce had been bitter, drawn out, and in the end, Beth had used every legal maneuver she could to take the kids and keep Daniel at a distance. He didn't have the money or the resources to fight her then, and with his life falling apart after losing his job, he had been too broken to stand up for himself. Beth had won, and Daniel was left on the streets—homeless, childless, and with nothing to show for the years he had tried to be a good husband and father. Now, as he stared at the message, those old wounds reopened. The kids—what did they think of him? Had Beth poisoned them against him all these years, or did they even remember him at all?

Angela leaned in, her voice softening. "You don't have to do this alone, you know."

Daniel looked up at her, grateful for her steady presence. Angela had been his anchor through so much. She'd found him at his lowest and lifted him up when he didn't think he could stand again. But this—this was something deeper, something he hadn't even let himself think about for years.

"I know," he said finally. "But I have to face it. I can't keep running from them."

Later that evening, after dinner, Daniel found himself walking alone down a quiet street near their home. The air was cool, and the dim street lights cast long shadows along the sidewalk. His mind was swirling with memories of his old life—images of Beth, the kids, and the home they once shared. He could still see the house in his mind: the worn white shutters, the oak tree in the front yard where he used to push the kids on a tire swing. Those days felt like a lifetime ago. As he walked, Daniel thought about the person he had been back then—young, driven, and naive. He had worked long hours cleaning buildings and managing his small business, always thinking that if he could just make enough money, everything would fall into place. But

Beth had been distant, growing more frustrated with him as time went on. She wanted excitement, passion, a life that didn't involve Daniel coming home late, smelling like bleach and floor polish. He remembered how the fights had escalated, how every conversation seemed to turn into a confrontation until one day, it all fell apart. Beth had found someone else. Daniel never met the guy—didn't care to. He was younger, carefree, and everything Daniel wasn't. And then, just like that, Beth had filed for divorce, leaving Daniel to fend for himself. Losing the house and the kids had broken something in him. That's when his spiral into homelessness had begun. He shook his head, trying to push the memories away, but they clung to him like the night air. Now, Beth wanted to talk, and Daniel couldn't shake the feeling that she wasn't reaching out because she had suddenly grown a conscience. No, there was something else at play here.

As Daniel's thoughts drifted back to his present troubles, he realized how deeply Eric's betrayal mirrored what he had gone through with Beth. Both had been trusted parts of his life—one a friend, the other a partner—and both had turned their backs on him when he needed them most. Eric's greed and underhanded tactics had driven a wedge between them in business, just as Beth's desires had in his marriage. Eric had always been the charismatic one, the kind of man who could walk into a room and instantly command attention. Back when they started their cleaning business together, Eric's charm had been their biggest asset, helping them secure contracts and partnerships that Daniel never would have gotten on his own. But behind the scenes, Eric had been making side deals, cutting Daniel out of profits, and eventually trying to take control of the entire company. When Daniel confronted him, Eric hadn't even denied it—he had just smiled, like it was all part of some game that Daniel was too naïve to understand. It had taken every ounce of strength Daniel had to walk away from that partnership. He had started over with nothing, and it was only by the grace of

God—and Angela—that he had been able to rebuild. But now, with Eric's lawsuit looming and Beth reaching out, it felt like his past was circling back, trying to pull him under again.

The next day, Daniel found himself sitting at a small café near downtown, nervously sipping a cup of coffee as he waited for Beth to arrive. He hadn't seen her in years, and the anticipation was gnawing at him. Would she be the same person he remembered? Or had time changed her, just as it had changed him? When Beth finally walked through the door, Daniel's breath caught in his throat. She looked different—older, more tired, but still carrying herself with the same air of confidence that had once drawn him to her. Her hair was shorter, and there were faint lines around her eyes, but she was still unmistakably Beth. She spotted him and walked over, her smile faint but polite. Daniel stood to greet her, unsure of whether to offer a hug or a handshake. In the end, they settled for an awkward, brief embrace before sitting down.

"Daniel," she said softly, her voice tinged with something he couldn't quite place—regret, maybe? Or just the weight of years gone by?

"Beth," he replied, equally uncertain of how to navigate this reunion.

They sat in silence for a moment, the noise of the café around them filling the awkward gap between their words.

"I wasn't sure you'd agree to meet me," Beth said finally, stirring her coffee.

"I wasn't sure either," Daniel admitted. "But when you mentioned the kids…"

Beth nodded, her expression softening. "That's why I'm here. We need to talk about them."

Daniel braced himself, not sure what to expect. He had always feared that she would turn his kids against him, tell them lies about why he hadn't been around. And now, here she was, reopening the wound that had never quite healed.

"They've been asking about you," Beth continued, her voice almost too calm. "Especially our oldest. She's been wanting to know why you haven't been around, why you didn't fight harder to see them."

The guilt hit Daniel like a sledgehammer. He had fought, at least at first. But between the legal fees, his homelessness, and Beth's refusal to let him near the kids, he had eventually given up. It wasn't a decision he was proud of, but it was one he had made out of sheer survival.

"I didn't think you wanted me around," Daniel said, his voice thick with emotion. "You made it clear that you and the kids were moving on."

Beth's eyes flickered with something—remorse? "I was angry, Daniel. Hurt. I said a lot of things back then that I probably shouldn't have. But the kids... they deserve to know their father."

Daniel swallowed hard, the weight of her words settling in. Could it be that simple? After all these years, was there still a chance to reconnect with his children?

But even as hope flickered in his chest, Daniel couldn't shake the feeling that there was more to this meeting than Beth was letting on.

Daniel watched Beth closely, sensing that something was simmering beneath her words. She had always been a master at playing her cards close to her chest, but years of living on the streets and rebuilding his life had given him a sharper sense for when someone wasn't telling the whole truth.

"So, you're telling me you want the kids to see me now? After all this time?" Daniel asked, his voice low and measured. He was careful not to let too much emotion creep in, not yet. "What's changed?"

Beth glanced down at her coffee cup, swirling the liquid absentmindedly as if gathering her thoughts. She took a deep breath before speaking.

"It's complicated, Daniel," she began, her eyes finally meeting his. "The kids have been asking about you, yes. They're older now, and they're starting to form their own opinions. I've tried to shield them from… everything. But it's getting harder."

Daniel raised an eyebrow, leaning back in his chair. "Harder? Why now?"

Beth hesitated, her fingers tightening around the cup. There it was—the crack in the armor. Daniel had known Beth long enough to recognize when she was wrestling with something difficult.

"I'm not going to lie to you," she said, her voice quieter now. "Things aren't as good as they used to be. Financially, I mean."

Daniel felt his stomach twist. He should have seen this coming. The Beth he knew had always been a planner, someone who weighed every angle before making a move. This wasn't just about the kids; it was about survival.

"I thought you left me for someone who was 'better,'" Daniel said, his voice tinged with bitterness. "That guy—what happened to him?"

Beth's face hardened for a moment, the brief vulnerability replaced by the defensive posture Daniel remembered all too well. "He's gone," she said flatly. "That was a long time ago."

Daniel almost laughed, but there was no humor in it. She had left him for a younger man, someone who had promised her a more exciting life, and now, here she was—alone and struggling. He had been at his lowest back then, homeless and without hope, while she had paraded around with her new lover. Now the tables had turned, and Beth was the one reaching out, but not out of some sudden desire for family unity.

She needed something.

"How bad is it?" Daniel asked, cutting to the heart of the matter. He didn't have the energy for games anymore. "The finances, I mean."

Beth's eyes flickered with frustration, but she answered, "Bad. The business I was working for shut down last year. It's been tough finding steady work since then. And the bills—they're piling up."

Daniel didn't say anything at first. He had worked so hard to get back on his feet after losing everything, and now the woman who had abandoned him when he was at his lowest was sitting across from him, asking for help without directly asking for it.

"What do you want from me, Beth?" Daniel asked bluntly. "Why now?"

She sighed, looking down at her hands. "I don't want your money, Daniel. But... I need help. The kids, they deserve to know you. And if you could... maybe help out with some of the expenses, we could figure things out."

Daniel clenched his jaw. It was always about money, wasn't it? The bitter taste of betrayal lingered in his mouth, but there was something else, too—guilt. He hadn't been there for his kids, and now they were caught in the middle.

Daniel couldn't help but think about the last time he had seen his children. They were so young then—just five and seven. He could still picture their little faces, wide-eyed and full of confusion when he had to leave. Beth had made sure it was clear: they were moving on, and there was no place for him in their new life. The court orders, the emotional battles—it had all felt impossible to fight against. His oldest, Sophie, had always been a quiet and thoughtful child, the type to sit in her room for hours, drawing or reading. She had his curiosity, always asking him questions about the world when he tucked her in at night. He remembered how her face would light up when he'd tell her stories, her little fingers clutching her blanket as she hung on every word. But after the divorce, Daniel hadn't seen that light in her eyes again. She was seven when they parted, and now… what was she? Fifteen? Sixteen? The idea that he had missed nearly a decade of her life gnawed at his insides. And then there was his youngest, Mason. A whirlwind of energy and laughter. When Daniel used to come home late from work, exhausted and beaten down from the grind, Mason was always the one who could lift his spirits. He was barely five when Daniel had to leave, and now… now he would be almost a teenager. Mason probably didn't even remember him—just a vague shadow in the background of his early childhood. The guilt was suffocating. He had tried to fight in the beginning, hiring lawyers he couldn't afford, but Beth had stacked the deck against him. Her new relationship, her financial stability, the house—it had all worked in her favor. And so Daniel, broken and defeated, had slowly drifted out of his children's lives.

Now, sitting across from Beth, it felt like all that pain and regret was rushing back. He had always told himself that he would make things right one day, but that day had never come. Until now.

"What have you told them about me?" Daniel asked quietly, his voice trembling slightly.

Beth hesitated again, and for the first time, Daniel saw a flicker of shame in her eyes. "I didn't lie to them, Daniel," she said, but there was a heaviness to her words. "I told them that you... weren't around because of your situation. That you were struggling."

Daniel's heart ached at the thought of his kids growing up thinking of him as a failure. Even if it was partly true, it wasn't the whole story. They hadn't seen the sleepless nights, the cold floors of the church back room, the endless hours of cleaning just to survive. They hadn't seen the man he had become, the man he was now.

"And what do they think?" Daniel pressed.

Beth shifted uncomfortably in her seat. "Sophie... she's angry. She doesn't understand why you didn't fight harder. She's smart, Daniel. She's grown up a lot, and she has a lot of questions. Mason, well, he's quieter about it, but I can tell he's curious. He wants to know who you are."

Daniel stared down at his hands, his chest tightening. How could he explain to them what had happened? How could he make them understand that he hadn't given up on them, even when the world had beaten him down?

"You said Sophie's angry," Daniel said after a pause. "Does she hate me?"

Beth looked away, biting her lip. "I don't think she hates you, but she's hurt. She's had to grow up fast, and in a lot of ways, she's taken on the role of being strong for Mason. She feels like she's had to take care of him because I've been working so much."

Daniel felt a wave of shame wash over him. His absence had forced Sophie to become someone she never should have had to be—stronger, harder. A protector when she should have just been a child.

"What about Mason?" Daniel asked, his voice barely above a whisper. "Does he even remember me?"

Beth hesitated again. "He remembers you, but… not much. It's like you're a story he's heard a few times, but he doesn't really know who you are. He's curious, Daniel. He's asked me questions, but I've never known what to say."

Daniel felt his heart break. His own son barely knew him, and now he was just a ghost of a memory. How could he ever fix that? As they sat in that café, the weight of everything that had been left unsaid over the years filled the space between them. Beth was asking for help, but Daniel knew it wasn't just about the money. It was about redemption—for him, for his children, and maybe even for her. Despite everything she had done, Beth was still the mother of his children, and there was a chance, however small, that they could find some way to mend the broken pieces of their lives.

"I need to think about all of this," Daniel said finally, his voice steady but distant. "But if I'm going to be in their lives, it has to be on the right terms. No more games, Beth. They deserve better than that."

Beth nodded, looking relieved. "I understand," she said softly. "I just want to do what's best for them."

Daniel stood up, ready to leave. "I'll be in touch," he said, his mind already churning with the possibilities ahead. Reconnecting with his kids would be the hardest thing he'd ever done, but if there was any chance to make things right, he had to take it.

Months passed, and just as Daniel had feared, Eric's threats escalated, spiraling swiftly into a relentless legal assault. Court filings began arriving in waves—accusations of breach of partnership, demands for a share of profits, claims of unethical business practices. Each new summons contained fresh grievances, all aimed at unearthing and exploiting every possible weak spot in Daniel's defenses. Eric had spared no expense, weaponizing the courts in his vendetta, and the sheer volume of the filings kept Daniel's legal team working tirelessly. They pored over every scrap of documentation, combing through years of records, emails, and contractual agreements from the time he'd severed ties with Eric, determined to lay bare Eric's manipulations and meticulously build Daniel's defense. From the outset, the case seemed daunting. Each court date was filled with Eric's grandstanding, his smug declarations spilling over with accusations and demands for documentation. His arrogance was unmistakable, his smirk in court a constant reminder that he believed he held the upper hand. He seemed to savor each chance to publicly tarnish Daniel's name, relishing the damage he could do to his former partner's reputation. But Daniel's attorney, a seasoned litigator well-versed in corporate disputes and no stranger to cases of deception, knew exactly where to dig. She took apart Eric's claims piece by piece, uncovering a pattern of misrepresentations that painted a starkly different picture of their past partnership. Hidden within years-old records were hints that Eric had, in fact, falsified key documents and manipulated contracts to divert company resources for personal gain. With every new discovery, the tide began to shift. Eric's once-ironclad case started to crack under the weight of mounting evidence against him. When Daniel finally took the stand, he spoke with a calm, steady voice that cut through the courtroom tension. He recounted the journey of building his business from the ground up, the years of hard work and integrity it had taken to restore his life and reputation after Eric's betrayal. His testimony was measured, unwavering, his words filled with the weight of truth. He detailed the sacrifices he'd made, the relentless commitment to rebuild everything that had been nearly lost when Eric's actions nearly destroyed him. There was no need for grand gestures or emotional pleas; his quiet resolve left little doubt about his honesty and dedication.

The turning point came during one pivotal hearing. Daniel's attorney presented a series of emails Eric had thought he'd erased long ago. These messages were damning, exposing a calculated plot from the very beginning—Eric's intentions to use Daniel's business as a temporary cash cow, exploiting it for profit before slipping away to new ventures. Line by line, the emails dismantled every claim Eric had made, laying bare his deceit and malice. The courtroom fell silent, the weight of Eric's own words unraveling his case. By the time the judge issued the final ruling, Eric's demeanor had shifted completely. Gone was the smirk, replaced with a look of defeat as the verdict was read aloud: Eric's claims were baseless, his actions malicious, and his behavior in the lawsuit nothing short of fraudulent. Not only was he awarded nothing from Daniel's business, but he was also ordered to cover restitution—reimbursing Daniel for legal expenses and the emotional toll his actions had inflicted.

Outside the courthouse, Daniel felt an almost palpable weight lift from his shoulders. Angela was waiting, a relieved smile breaking across her face as she saw him emerge. They embraced quietly, a moment of shared relief washing over them. For the first time in months, it felt like the cloud of Eric's influence had finally dissipated, the threat he had posed now a memory. In an unexpected turn, the fallout from Eric's defeat rippled through the business community. Word spread quickly about his failed lawsuit, the revelations about his deception marking him as a liability no reputable firm wanted to touch. His once-solid reputation was now in tatters, weighed down by debt and mounting legal fees. Meanwhile, Daniel emerged from the battle unscathed, his business fortified and his reputation stronger than ever. Walking away from the courthouse that day, Daniel felt a profound sense of closure. The last remnant of his troubled past with Eric was now behind him, the burden of those old ties finally severed. He had come out the other side with his integrity, his family, and the life he had worked so hard to rebuild. Whatever came next, he knew he was ready, this time with no one standing in his way.

CHAPTER 10

Daniel sat in his truck, eyes fixed on the house where his children lived. It wasn't anything remarkable, just an older suburban home—modest and worn, its age visible in the faded paint and sagging gutters, signs of a house that had been lived in but not meticulously cared for. The front yard, once probably neat and well-kept, now had patches of dry grass mixed with overgrown weeds, a swing set tilted slightly to one side as if years of use and neglect had left their mark. The familiarity of the scene tugged at something inside him, a bittersweet reminder of a life that could have been. His hand gripped the steering wheel, knuckles whitening as a subtle tremor passed through his fingers. He took a deep breath, trying to summon the courage to open the door, to step outside and face a reality that felt more daunting than any confrontation he'd had before. Nearly a decade had passed since he'd been this close to them. Almost ten years of absence, of missed birthdays, school events, and quiet moments he would never get back. The weight of it all settled heavily on his chest, making it harder to breathe. He thought about the phone call from earlier that week. His voice had been shaky, unsteady, as he forced himself to ask Beth if he could see them— Sophie and Mason. He could still hear the hesitation in her voice, the pause that felt like it stretched out forever. She hadn't said yes right away. There had been a moment, a long silence where he imagined she was weighing the damage, wondering if it was worth opening old wounds. But in the end, she agreed.

"Come by after school," she had said. He remembered how her voice softened just slightly when she added, "It's better if they're both home."

The names echoed in his mind: Sophie and Mason. How long had it been since he'd said their names out loud? Years, at least. He tried to picture their faces, to mentally reconstruct the children he had once known, but time had warped those memories. Sophie, who had once been small enough to sit on his shoulders, and Mason, barely walking when he left—now they were almost strangers. Older, taller, with new experiences, new memories that didn't include him. His mind grasped at fragments of the past, but the images were blurry, like photographs left out in the sun too long. Another deep breath. His hand moved to the door handle, and with a slow, deliberate motion, he pushed it open. The cool air hit him as he stepped out onto the pavement. His legs felt heavy, as if each step toward the house dragged behind it the weight of all the time he had lost. Thoughts churned in his mind, competing for his attention—what he would say, how they might react, whether they even wanted to see him. Beth had rejected him all those years ago, her anger sharp and unforgiving, and now the fear of facing that same cold dismissal from his own children gnawed at him. He had missed so much, abandoned so much. They had grown up without him, and the gap between them felt as vast and impossible to cross as an ocean. But here he was, standing at the front door. The dull thud of his heart pounded in his ears, his pulse quickening with each passing second. His instinct was to run, to retreat back to the safety of the truck, to let the distance between them remain unchallenged. But deep down, he knew he couldn't. Not anymore. The years of silence had stretched too long. He owed them more than just his presence. He owed them the chance to confront him, to ask questions he knew they had. And even if the answers weren't easy or the reunion wasn't kind, he owed them at least that. Before he could second-guess himself, before the rising tide of doubt could drown him, Daniel raised his fist and knocked on the door.

A few moments passed before the door creaked open. Standing there, taller than he remembered, was Sophie. She had grown so much—no longer the small, wide-eyed girl he used to carry on his shoulders but now a young woman with a posture that exuded a guarded confidence. Her face, however, was unreadable, a mask of indifference that chilled him more than any words could. For a long moment, neither of them spoke, the silence heavy and oppressive between them.

"Hi, Sophie," Daniel finally managed, his voice strained, the tightness in his chest making it hard to get the words out. He wanted to say more, to explain himself somehow, but the words stuck in his throat. How could he summarize nearly ten years of absence in a greeting? How could he begin to convey everything he had been through, everything he had missed?

Sophie crossed her arms over her chest, the motion quick and defensive, as if bracing herself for whatever was about to happen. Her gaze was hard, eyes sharp and cold. "Mom said you were coming," she said flatly, the words devoid of any warmth or emotion. It was a statement, not an invitation. There was no joy, no relief at seeing him—just the acknowledgment that his presence had been foretold and now it had to be endured.

Daniel swallowed hard, feeling the weight of her coldness press down on him like a physical force. He had anticipated this, had told himself over and over that he couldn't expect anything more, but the sting of her distance was sharper than he'd imagined. The pain was like a slow burn, steady and relentless. He nodded, trying to keep his expression neutral, trying not to let the hurt show.

"Yeah," he said, his voice more tentative than he intended. "I wanted to see you and Mason… if that's okay."

Sophie didn't reply immediately. She stood there for a few beats, her eyes narrowing slightly as if she were weighing whether to let him in or send him away. Finally, without a word, she stepped back and pulled the door open wider, an unspoken permission that came without enthusiasm. It wasn't forgiveness, but it was something.

Daniel hesitated for a second, then stepped inside, feeling an overwhelming sense of unease settle over him. The house had a strange duality—both foreign and familiar. It had the typical clutter of a lived-in home: shoes haphazardly piled by the entrance, a jacket carelessly thrown over the back of a dining chair, schoolbooks scattered across the kitchen table as if abandoned mid-study. But there was also something off about the place, an underlying tension, like everything was on the verge of unraveling. He could sense it, the strain in the air, the way the house seemed to hold its breath now that he was inside.

His eyes scanned the room briefly before landing on Mason, who had appeared silently in the doorway to the living room. The boy was almost unrecognizable—no longer the little kid he remembered. He was taller now, his limbs awkward and gangly as though he hadn't quite grown into them yet. There was a hint of adolescence in his face, a mixture of curiosity and wariness, but he didn't approach. He hung back, observing, his posture stiff like he didn't quite know where he belonged in this moment.

"Mason," Daniel said, his voice thick with emotion as he took in the sight of his son. He had tried to imagine what Mason would look like after all these years, but the reality of seeing him—so changed, so unfamiliar—hit him harder than he expected. He was no longer the little boy who used to sit on his lap or race toy cars across the kitchen floor. Now, he was a stranger, someone Daniel didn't know how to reach.

Mason stared at him, his expression a mix of uncertainty and something else Daniel couldn't quite read. There was a tension in his jaw, a hesitance in his posture that suggested he wasn't sure how to feel. The silence stretched between them, thick and uncomfortable, before Mason finally spoke, his voice low and cautious. "Hey."

It was just a single word, barely more than an acknowledgment, but it was a start. Daniel held onto it, even though the gap between them still felt enormous. It was something to cling to, something that might eventually grow into more. But for now, he understood that this was all they could manage. Neither of them knew how to bridge the years of separation, but at least they were standing on the same side of the door.

The conversation that followed was strained, halting. Daniel asked them about school, about what they liked to do, trying to find some thread of common ground to grasp onto. Sophie's answers were clipped, guarded, while Mason responded more out of politeness than interest. They were still sizing him up, unsure of who this man was who had appeared after all these years. Daniel wanted to tell them everything—about how hard it had been, how much he had missed them, how often he had thought of them over the years. But the words felt too heavy, too complicated for this fragile moment. Instead, he listened more than he spoke, trying to piece together the lives they had lived without him. Sophie was in high school now, taking advanced classes and talking about colleges. She had always been smart, but hearing her talk about her ambitions made Daniel realize just how much he had missed. She had become her own person, independent and strong-willed, and Daniel could sense the resentment simmering beneath her calm exterior. Mason was quieter, still trying to figure out who he was in the world. He talked about his friends, about video games and sports, but there was a distance in his tone, like he wasn't sure how much to share with this stranger sitting in his living room. Daniel could feel the walls they had built around themselves, and he knew it would take time to break through them. But at least he was here. At least he had this chance. Over the next few weeks, Daniel began to spend more time with his children. It wasn't easy. Every visit felt like walking on eggshells, with Sophie's guarded responses and Mason's quiet detachment. Beth was usually in the background, keeping her distance but always watching, as though waiting to see if Daniel would mess up. He couldn't help but wonder what Beth had told them about him over the years. He could see the way Sophie looked at him, like she was waiting for him to fail, to prove that he wasn't the father she had needed. Mason was more neutral, but there was still a barrier there, a sense of uncertainty about whether or not to trust him.

One evening, after the kids had gone to bed, Daniel stayed behind to talk to Beth. It was the first time they had been alone since their initial meeting at the café.

"You told them I didn't fight for them," Daniel said quietly, leaning against the kitchen counter.

Beth didn't look at him at first. She was rinsing dishes at the sink, her movements slow and deliberate. "I told them the truth, Daniel," she replied, her voice calm but cold.

"That's not the whole truth," he said, his frustration building. "You made it sound like I just walked away."

Beth turned to face him, her expression hard. "You did walk away. You didn't have a choice, but that doesn't change what happened. You weren't there, and I had to explain that to them."

Daniel's fists clenched at his sides, the anger he had been holding back for years bubbling to the surface. "I was homeless, Beth. I didn't have anything. You think I didn't want to be there for them? I fought as hard as I could."

She sighed, her shoulders slumping slightly. For the first time, Daniel saw a flicker of vulnerability in her eyes. "I know, Daniel," she said softly. "I know you were struggling. But they needed stability, and I had to make choices."

There was a long pause, the weight of their shared history hanging in the air between them.

"You hurt them, Daniel," Beth said quietly. "Whether it was your fault or not, you hurt them. And it's going to take time for them to trust you again."

Daniel felt the sting of her words, but he knew she was right. He had hurt them, even if he hadn't meant to. And now, it was his job to rebuild what had been broken. As the months passed, Daniel slowly began to mend the fractured relationship with his children. It wasn't perfect—there were still moments of tension, moments where the past reared its ugly head—but they were starting to trust him again. Sophie began to open up more, sharing her dreams and frustrations with him, and Mason started to talk to him like a friend, not just a distant figure from his past. Angela was a constant source of support during this time. She never pushed or prodded, but she was always there when Daniel needed someone to talk to, someone to help him process the emotional weight of rebuilding his family. She had come to understand that this journey was not just about Daniel and his children—it was about healing the wounds of the past and finding a way forward together.

And yet, in the back of Daniel's mind, he knew that there was one more challenge to face. Daniel had thought about it many times over the past few months. Beth had been civil with him, cooperative even, but there was always an undercurrent of tension. She had lost her financial footing, and though she hadn't directly asked him for money since that day in the café, Daniel knew it was only a matter of time before the subject came up again. But what he hadn't anticipated was the other shoe dropping. He hadn't expected his ex-wife to come back, not after everything they had been through. It was a Wednesday evening when Beth called him, her voice tight with something he couldn't quite place.

"We need to talk," she said. "It's about the kids… and about custody."

Daniel felt his stomach drop. He had fought so hard to reconnect with Sophie and Mason, to build something real with them. Now, it seemed like Beth was preparing to challenge that. Whatever this was about, it wouldn't be easy. As he hung up the phone, Daniel's mind raced with the possibilities. The thought of losing his children again, just when they were starting to trust him, was almost unbearable. He knew he had to face whatever was coming, but this time, he wouldn't be alone. He had Angela by his side, and for the first time in a long time, he felt ready to fight for what mattered most.

It was a Wednesday evening when Beth called him, her voice tight and clipped. There had been little conversation between them recently beyond the logistics of Sophie and Mason's lives, but this call felt different, more ominous.

"We need to talk," Beth said flatly. "It's about the kids... and custody."

Daniel froze, the words sinking in like a punch to the gut. Custody? After all this time? His heart raced, and for a moment, he thought he hadn't heard her right.

"What do you mean, custody?" he asked, his voice strained. "Why now?"

Beth sighed on the other end, and there was a pause. He could almost picture her sitting on the other side, maybe at the kitchen table, tapping her fingers in that impatient way she always had.

"I can't afford this anymore, Daniel," she said, her tone sharp with frustration. "Raising two kids on a single income while you're living your new life—away from them—hasn't been easy. Mason needs tutoring, and Sophie's got her extracurriculars. I can't do it all on my own. I need more help... or I'll need more control over their lives. Custody needs to be reconsidered."

Daniel clenched his jaw. He had been fighting so hard to rebuild his relationship with Sophie and Mason, and just as things were beginning to settle, Beth was threatening to rip it all away. He felt the familiar swirl of anger and fear rising in his chest, but he swallowed it down, forcing himself to stay calm.

"I've been here, Beth," he said firmly. "I've been showing up. Sophie and Mason are starting to trust me again. You can't just—"

"I'm not trying to take them away from you," she interrupted, her voice softening, but not enough to hide the underlying tension. "But things need to change. I need financial support, and if that means taking this to court, then..."

Beth trailed off, leaving the unsaid threat hanging in the air.

Daniel sat in silence for a long while after the call ended, staring blankly at the phone in his hand. His mind raced through all the possibilities—the legal battles, the tension it would create between him and the kids, the strain it would put on his relationship with Angela. He knew Beth wasn't bluffing; if she had decided to pursue this, there was no backing down. Later that night, Daniel shared the news with Angela. They sat together on their porch, the cool evening air brushing against their faces. Angela leaned back in her chair, her hands wrapped around a mug of tea, her eyes filled with concern.

"Are you sure she's serious about custody?" Angela asked gently. "Do you think she's just trying to scare you into giving her money?"

Daniel rubbed his face, feeling the weight of the situation pressing down on him. "Maybe. But I can't risk it. If she files for full custody, it'll be a nightmare. Sophie and Mason are finally starting to open up to me again. I can't lose them."

Angela nodded, her eyes thoughtful. "Then we fight. You've worked too hard to let this slip away. And we'll figure out the money part."

She reached over, placing her hand on his. "I've been with you every step of the way, Daniel. We're not going to lose them."

Her words were a comfort, but Daniel knew that the road ahead wouldn't be easy. They would have to navigate the complexities of Beth's demands, the legal implications, and most importantly, the emotional toll it would take on everyone involved.

Over the following days, Daniel tried to stay focused on the time he had with Sophie and Mason. He could sense the unease in Sophie, especially, who had overheard a phone conversation between Beth and one of her friends. Sophie was now old enough to understand that something was going on, and it showed in the way she looked at Daniel, with those same questioning eyes she had when she was younger.

"Dad," Sophie asked one evening after dinner, as she was helping him clean up. "Is something wrong? Mom's been weird lately, and I heard her talking about court."

Daniel hesitated, not wanting to burden her with too much. But she was nearly a teenager now, and shielding her from the truth would only backfire.

"Your mom and I are working through some things," he said carefully. "We're trying to figure out what's best for you and Mason."

Sophie frowned, her eyes narrowing. "Does that mean we'll have to go to court?"

Daniel placed a hand on her shoulder. "I don't know yet, but I promise you this: no matter what happens, I'll always be here for you and your brother. Nothing's going to change that."

She nodded, but Daniel could see the uncertainty lingering in her eyes. She had grown up too fast, forced to navigate the fractured dynamics between her parents. Mason, on the other hand, seemed blissfully unaware of the tension.

A few days later, Daniel received a call on his mobile phone that sat on his work table, vibrating. Daniel's hand tightened around the phone as the voice on the other end trembled, filling his ears with words he didn't want to hear. Time seemed to slow down, each word seeping into his bones, heavy and suffocating.

"There's been an accident... Beth... car crash... she's gone, Daniel."

Gone.

For a moment, Daniel just stood there in the middle of his workshop, the hum of the machines fading to a distant background noise. His heart pounded so hard in his chest that he could feel it in his throat, the blood rushing to his head. He gripped the edge of the workbench, trying to keep himself upright as the weight of the news hit him with brutal force.

"Are the kids okay?" His voice was hoarse, barely a whisper, as if speaking louder would shatter whatever thin thread was holding him together.

"They're fine," the neighbor reassured him, though her voice wavered. "They weren't with her. They're at school, waiting to be picked up... I—I thought you should know right away."

Daniel nodded even though no one could see him, his mind racing to keep up. Beth was gone. The woman he had spent so many years fighting, hating, forgiving, and co-parenting with was just... gone. And Sophie, Mason—his children—were about to lose the most constant person in their lives.

The phone slipped from his hand and clattered onto the workbench, the call still open but forgotten. Daniel stared blankly at the wood grains beneath his fingers, his breath shallow, as if the world had suddenly shrunk into something smaller, more fragile. Daniel didn't remember grabbing his keys or shutting down the workshop. The drive to the hospital was a blur of red lights and swerving traffic, the pounding in his chest only growing louder as he gripped the steering wheel. His knuckles were white, his vision tunneled, and the sky outside had darkened with thick, low clouds that threatened rain. He tried to focus on the road, but his thoughts were a storm of memories. Flashes of Beth from years ago, before everything had fallen apart—their wedding day, the early years when they were still hopeful. Her laugh, the way she used to toss her hair over her shoulder, her eyes fierce when they argued, but always filled with a determined fire. She had been his world, once.

And now, she was gone.

His thoughts shifted to Sophie and Mason. How would he tell them? How could he look into their innocent faces and tell them that their mother—the woman who had been there for every scraped knee, every school play, every bedtime story— wasn't coming back? His hands trembled on the wheel as the full gravity of it settled over him.

CHAPTER 11

The hospital was a maze of sterile hallways and the faint smell of antiseptic. The lights overhead flickered slightly, casting everything in a cold, almost surreal glow. Daniel walked through the doors like a man in a daze, his legs feeling like they might give out at any moment. The nurse behind the desk glanced up, her face softening immediately when she saw him.

"Daniel Hamilton?" she asked gently, already knowing why he was there.

He nodded, barely able to form words. "Beth... Beth Hamilton. Where is she?"

The nurse's eyes flickered with sympathy, and she motioned for him to follow her. As they walked through the hallways, Daniel felt each step grow heavier, as if the weight of what was coming was pressing him into the ground. He wasn't sure he could handle it. But he kept going, because he had to.

The nurse led him to a quiet room off the main corridor, the walls painted a muted gray. It felt far too serene for what he knew was about to happen. Inside, a doctor stood waiting, his expression somber. He introduced himself, but Daniel didn't hear the name. His ears were ringing, his body cold despite the warmth of the room.

"I'm sorry, Mr. Hamilton," the doctor began. "There was nothing we could do. The impact—" He hesitated, glancing down at the chart in his hand as if the words would be easier to say if he wasn't looking at Daniel. "She died on impact. She didn't suffer."

Didn't suffer. The words echoed in Daniel's mind, but they brought no comfort. How could there be comfort in this? The woman he had spent years of his life with, the mother of his children, was gone, and it had happened so suddenly, so violently.

"Can I see her?" he asked, his voice cracking.

The doctor nodded, stepping aside to let Daniel into the room.

When Daniel stepped inside, the room was quiet, almost eerily so. Beth lay on the bed, her body covered by a thin white sheet, her face pale and serene. For a moment, Daniel couldn't move. He stood frozen, staring at her like she might wake up, like this might all be some horrible mistake. But it wasn't. She was gone. He took a step closer, his heart pounding in his chest. Her face looked so different now, drained of life, but there were still traces of the woman he had once loved. The sharp lines of her jaw, the curve of her lips, the faint freckles across her cheeks that she had always hated but he had adored. The memories flooded in—so many moments they had shared, the good and the bad. The nights spent laughing over wine, the mornings arguing over burnt toast. The joy they had felt when Sophie was born, and later Mason. The slow unraveling of their marriage, the bitterness that had taken root, the resentment that had grown between them like a wall. But now, standing here, none of that mattered. All the anger, the hurt, the years of estrangement— they all seemed so small in the face of this finality.

"I'm sorry," he whispered, his voice barely audible. His eyes burned, but no tears came. "I'm so sorry."

He reached out, his fingers trembling as they brushed against her hand, cold and lifeless beneath his touch. He stayed there for a long time, the silence pressing in on him, the weight of everything they had been, and everything they had lost, hanging heavy in the air.

The hardest part was yet to come. Leaving the hospital was like stepping into a different world—one that was still moving forward, oblivious to the fact that everything had just changed for him, for Sophie, for Mason. The sky had darkened, and fat drops of rain were starting to fall, splattering against the windshield as Daniel drove toward their school. His mind was spinning, grasping for the right words, but none came.

How could he tell them that their mother was gone? How could he be the one to take away their sense of safety, their innocence?

He arrived at the school, the rain now pouring down in heavy sheets. He saw Sophie and Mason standing under the awning near the entrance, backpacks slung over their small shoulders, their faces lighting up when they spotted him. They ran toward him, eager to escape the storm, their voices overlapping as they talked about their day.

"Dad! You're here early!" Mason grinned, oblivious to the dark cloud hanging over Daniel.

Sophie, older and more perceptive, frowned, noticing the tension in his face. "Dad... what's wrong?"

Daniel knelt down, his heart breaking into a million pieces as he looked into their wide, innocent eyes. He took a deep breath, trying to steady himself, but the words felt like knives in his throat.

"There's something I need to tell you," he said softly, his voice trembling. He looked at Sophie, then Mason. "Mom... Mom had an accident. She's—"

The words hung in the air, heavy and suffocating. For a moment, neither of them moved, the shock freezing them in place. Then, slowly, reality began to sink in.

"No…" Mason's voice was small, confused. "What do you mean, gone?"

Sophie's face crumpled as she realized the truth. She let out a small, broken sob and threw herself into Daniel's arms, her body shaking. Mason, still too young to fully grasp it, stood there, his face blank with disbelief.

Daniel held them both close, his heart shattering as they cried. He wanted to protect them from this pain, to take it all away, but there was nothing he could do. All he could do was hold them and promise that, somehow, they would get through this together. At that moment, Daniel realized that everything had changed. He was no longer the man trying to rebuild his life. He was now a father, alone, with two children who needed him more than ever. Daniel's hand tightened around the phone as the voice on the other end trembled, filling his ears with words he didn't want to hear. Time seemed to slow down, each word seeping into his bones, heavy and suffocating.

The days following Beth's death were a blur of grief and arrangements. The house felt hollow and cold, filled with the echoes of memories that now seemed distant and painful. Daniel struggled to balance his own sorrow with the needs of Sophie and Mason. They were lost, their mother ripped from their lives without warning, and they clung to Daniel like a lifeline. The funeral was a somber affair, attended by family, friends, and the community. Angela stood by Daniel's side, a pillar of strength, her presence a constant reminder that life, despite its cruelty, could still offer moments of grace. Sophie and Mason clutched each other's hands, their faces pale and tear-streaked, their eyes searching the crowd for something familiar, something safe. In the weeks that followed, Daniel had to learn how to be both mother and father. He found himself struggling to fill the void left by Beth, trying to manage the household, his business, and the emotional needs of his children. There were moments when the weight of it all felt unbearable, when he wondered if he could ever truly be enough for them. But he wasn't alone. Angela was there, helping him navigate this new reality. She stepped in without hesitation, picking up where Beth had left off, not as a replacement but as a support. She helped with school runs, meals, and the thousand small things that kept the household running. Her quiet strength and unwavering faith became a beacon for Daniel, guiding him through the darkest days. Eventually, Daniel and the children moved all of their belongings out of Beth's house and lived exclusively with Angela.

One evening, after the children were asleep, Angela and Daniel sat together on the porch, the cool night air a soothing balm. Angela looked at Daniel, her eyes filled with a mix of sadness and determination.

"Daniel, I need to tell you something," she said softly, her voice steady but her hands trembling slightly.

Daniel turned to her, concern etched on his face. "What is it, Angela?"

"I've been to the doctor," she began, taking a deep breath. "I've been having some health issues, and they've run some tests."

Daniel's heart skipped a beat, a cold fear settling in his stomach. "What did they say?"

Angela reached for his hand, her grip firm. "They found something, a tumor. It's small, and they believe they caught it early, but I'm going to need treatment. I don't want to hide this from you, especially now. You and the kids need to know what's happening."

The words hit Daniel like a physical blow. The thought of losing Angela, after everything they had already been through, was unbearable. But looking into her eyes, he saw a strength and resolve that gave him hope.

"We'll get through this," he said, his voice firm despite the fear gnawing at him. "Whatever it takes, we'll get through it together."

As Angela began her treatment, the family settled into a new rhythm. It wasn't easy, but they found a way to make it work. Daniel juggled his responsibilities, finding solace in the routine of work and the love of his children. Sophie and Mason slowly began to heal, their laughter returning, though tinged with the loss they had experienced. Angela's treatments were tough, but she faced them with the same determination that had guided her through life. Daniel was by her side every step of the way, offering his unwavering support. He admired her courage, her faith, and the way she continued to find joy in the smallest of things, even on the hardest days. Through it all, the bond between Daniel and Angela grew stronger. They found comfort in each other, a shared strength that helped them face each new challenge. Angela's illness brought them closer, deepening their connection and solidifying their commitment to each other and to the family they were building. One afternoon, as Daniel was closing up his workshop, he saw a figure standing at the edge of the driveway. As the person stepped forward, Daniel recognized him instantly—his old business partner, Marcus. Marcus had been a part of Daniel's life during some of his darkest times, their partnership dissolving under the weight of Daniel's personal struggles. Seeing him now, after so many years, brought a flood of mixed emotions.

"Marcus," Daniel greeted him, his voice cautious. "What brings you here?"

Marcus shifted uncomfortably, his eyes darting around. "I heard about Beth. I'm sorry, Daniel. Truly."

Daniel nodded, the pain still fresh. "Thank you. It's been... a lot to handle."

Marcus looked at him, a hint of regret in his eyes. "I know we didn't part on the best terms, but I've been thinking a lot about what happened. I've been working on myself, trying to make amends where I can. I wanted to reach out, see if we could talk."

Daniel studied him, unsure of what to say. The memories of their last days as partners were still raw, but there was something different about Marcus now—a sincerity that Daniel hadn't seen before.

"Alright," Daniel said finally. "Let's talk."

Their conversation was long and filled with apologies, confessions, and a mutual desire to move forward. Marcus explained how he had sought therapy, worked through his own issues, and realized the mistakes he had made. He expressed a genuine desire to make things right, not just with Daniel but with himself. For Daniel, it was a chance to confront his own past, to let go of the lingering bitterness and embrace forgiveness. He found himself opening up, sharing his journey, the struggles, and the triumphs. It was cathartic, a release of years of pent-up emotions. In the end, they agreed to give their partnership another chance. It wouldn't be easy, but they were both committed to making it work. Marcus's return brought a new sense of purpose to Daniel's life, a reminder that even the deepest wounds could heal with time and effort. With Marcus back in the picture and Angela's health steadily improving, Daniel found himself looking toward the future with renewed hope. The cleaning business was thriving, and with Marcus's help, they began exploring new opportunities, expanding their reach and taking on bigger projects. Angela, too, found strength in her work. Despite the challenges of her treatment, she continued to design, her creativity a beacon of light in the darkness. Her fashion line for plus-size women was gaining recognition, and she poured her heart into every piece, drawing inspiration from her journey and the people she loved.

Sophie and Mason adapted to their new life, their resilience shining through. They missed their mother, but they found comfort in the love and support of their father and Angela. When Daniel first introduced Angela to his children, Sophie and Mason, the meeting was tentative, even strained. Sophie, the older of the two, watched Angela with guarded eyes, sizing her up with the quiet skepticism of a child who had been hurt before. Mason was less reserved, but his shyness made him cling to his sister, clearly uncertain about Angela's place in their lives. Angela, sensing their hesitance, kept her distance, engaging with them without pushing too hard, her patience as gentle as it was intentional. In the beginning, Angela's attempts to connect were met with polite indifference. She tried finding common ground, asking Sophie about her favorite books and Mason about his toys. But Sophie gave curt answers, while Mason remained shy, nodding or shrugging without much enthusiasm. For the first few visits, Angela could feel the kids drawing lines around themselves, keeping her out as they clung to each other and the safety of their routine.

Angela took it in stride, though. She didn't try to force herself into their world. Instead, she observed, quietly learning what brought each of them comfort, where they felt happiest, and what topics sparked their interest. She noticed that Sophie often buried herself in novels, preferring fantasy books with strong female leads. Mason, on the other hand, had a fascination with building things, often getting lost in his blocks and toy trains, meticulously crafting structures that, while simple, had the focused precision of someone who enjoyed making things fit.

Gradually, Angela found small ways to connect with them, meeting them where they were instead of drawing them into her world. One day, she came over with a gift for Sophie—a book she had handpicked, one with a plot similar to the ones Sophie often read. She handed it to her casually, not making a big deal about it, simply saying she thought Sophie might like it. Sophie took the book with a skeptical look, but Angela caught a glimmer of interest in her eyes. Later, when she spotted Sophie reading it in a corner, deeply engrossed, Angela felt her first small victory. With Mason, Angela took a different approach. She brought over a small building kit, nothing too elaborate, just something she thought he might enjoy. She showed him the kit but didn't try to assemble it for him, instead asking if he might show her how he would build something with it. At first, Mason was hesitant, but Angela's genuine curiosity and willingness to follow his lead slowly drew him out. He started showing her his structures, explaining why each piece went where it did, and she listened, her interest unfeigned, quietly applauding his creativity and letting him teach her.

As days turned into weeks, these small gestures began to add up. Sophie started asking Angela if she knew of other books she might like, even engaging in brief conversations about her favorite stories. Angela, thrilled by this small breakthrough, continued to feed Sophie's interests, giving her more recommendations and even discussing the books together. Their conversations deepened, with Sophie gradually opening up, sharing bits of her life and school experiences. Angela offered her gentle guidance when Sophie sought advice, subtly blending the line between friendly and parental, careful not to overstep her bounds. Mason, meanwhile, began to seek Angela out whenever she visited, eager to show her his latest creation or to see if she had brought any new building challenges. They developed a quiet camaraderie, often sitting side by side on the floor, working on little projects, laughing when things toppled over and celebrating when they succeeded.

Angela began introducing Sophie to the world of fashion design with a gentle, thoughtful approach, sensing the young girl's quiet curiosity about her work. It started one afternoon when Sophie asked Angela about the sketches scattered across her desk—rough outlines of dresses, jackets, and patterns filled with colors and notes. Angela, thrilled by Sophie's interest, pulled up a stool and began explaining the basics of sketching designs, showing her how she turned an idea into a wearable piece of art. Each visit after that, Angela would teach Sophie a new element of the craft. One day, it was fabrics—Angela introduced her to silk, linen, cotton, and wool, explaining how each material could make a piece feel different, look unique, and evoke a particular style. Sophie's eyes lit up as she touched each sample, marveling at the way they draped, feeling the difference between soft cashmere and sturdy denim. Another day, they explored color theory, with Angela showing her how certain shades could bring out a fabric's richness or change the entire mood of a piece. As Sophie's curiosity grew, Angela gave her small, age-appropriate tasks. She'd ask Sophie's opinion on color choices or let her try her hand at arranging swatches for a design mood board. When Sophie grew more confident, Angela introduced her to basic sketches, guiding her through the process of creating her own little designs—simple dresses or scarves—praising her creativity and helping her refine the details. Over time, Sophie became more comfortable, asking thoughtful questions, experimenting with colors, and learning to see clothing as art. Angela encouraged her to see fashion design as a form of self-expression, an outlet for creativity that had no limits. Their bond deepened through these quiet, shared moments in the studio, with Angela not only teaching her about art but also encouraging Sophie to find her own voice in her work.

Mason began to light up around her, his usual reserve melting away as he grew comfortable, trusting that Angela genuinely valued his thoughts and ideas. But the real turning point came on a Saturday afternoon when Daniel, Angela, Sophie, and Mason decided to spend the day together at the local park. Daniel had mentioned the trip in passing, expecting it to be an easy outing, but on the drive there, both Sophie and Mason seemed unusually quiet, a heaviness hanging in the air. Angela sensed their unease and suggested an impromptu picnic by the lake instead of staying near the bustling playground. Daniel agreed, and they spread out blankets near a quieter spot, unpacking sandwiches, fruit, and snacks they had brought along.

As they ate, Sophie quietly mentioned that their mother used to take them to the same park. Angela didn't pry; instead, she simply listened as Sophie shared memories of previous visits, with Mason chiming in about the games they used to play. Sensing this was a vulnerable moment for them, Angela remained respectful, asking only gentle questions, and in turn, sharing a few stories from her own childhood. Over the course of that afternoon, the walls between Angela and the children began to crumble. Sophie opened up more, talking freely and even laughing at a few of Angela's lighthearted jokes. Mason showed Angela his favorite tree, which he loved to climb, and to their surprise, Angela joined him, laughing as she carefully made her way up the lower branches. The kids were delighted, their laughter echoing across the lake as Angela playfully challenged Mason to a 'tree-sitting contest.'

That night, after they returned home, Sophie gave Angela an unexpected hug, whispering a quiet "thank you" before heading to her room. It was a small gesture, but it carried a weight that Angela didn't take lightly.

From that day on, Sophie and Mason treated Angela with a warmth they had previously reserved for family. She became their confidante, the one they turned to when they needed advice, encouragement, or simply someone to talk to. Angela took on the role with patience and grace, balancing discipline with kindness, and never pushing too hard. She respected their space but made it clear that she was there for them in every way that mattered. In time, they began inviting her into their lives willingly—Sophie, with her heartwarming stories of school and friends, and Mason, with his latest building project that he was eager to show off. Angela attended school events, cheered at their activities, and became a constant, supportive presence. Slowly but surely, she became more than just Daniel's partner; she became an essential part of their family, loved and accepted in a way that was genuine and lasting. Sophie and Mason knew, deep down, that Angela was someone they could trust, a steady presence who, no matter what, was there to stay.

After Beth's passing, Daniel decided they wouldn't move into her house. Instead, he chose to keep it exactly as it was — a tribute to her life, a memory palace filled with the details she had so carefully crafted. He continued paying the mortgage, treating it almost as a second home, though he and the children rarely visited. Beth's belongings remained untouched: her books lined the shelves, her clothes hung neatly in the closet, and her favorite mug sat on the kitchen counter, just as she had left it. Every corner of the house held something that reminded Daniel of her—the gentle colors she'd painted on the walls, the well-loved furniture, the tiny marks on the doorframe where she'd measured Sophie and Mason's growth over the years. Daniel knew that, for him and the kids, this space served as a sanctuary of memories, preserving Beth's essence. Though life moved forward in their own home, Beth's house would stay as she left it, a place they could visit whenever they wanted to feel her presence, her warmth, and the moments they had shared.